Unending Hope

Rebekah Lee Garris

PublishAmerica
Baltimore

ISBN: 1-4137-6776-1
PUBLISHED BY PUBLISHAMERICA, LLLP
www.publishamerica.com
Baltimore

Printed in the United States of America

Dedicated to my family

Table of Contents

CHAPTER ONE

April 14, 1865

Jolene Culhaine heard the horse being led into the barn. From where she sat in the hayloft, she couldn't see who it was, but she could guess that it was Elizabeth, her younger sister. The girls were two years apart, Jolene being fourteen.

Shutting the sketchbook she'd been drawing in, Jolene crawled over to the ladder and scrambled down.

Elizabeth was putting the horse away.

"How was school?" Jolene asked.

This was the first year that Jolene wasn't at the small, one-room schoolhouse in Crowfeather, Colorado. Elizabeth took Davie, who was eleven; Martha, who was nine; and Sammie, who was six, to school.

Elizabeth turned toward Jolene and brushed a strand of light brown hair out of her blue-gray eyes. Her lower lip quivered. "Awful. They made fun of us same as last year." A tear made its way slowly down her cheek. "'ceptin' this year, there's no one to stand up for us."

Jolene put an arm around her. "I know," she said. "I'm sorry."

The two girls looked very different as they stood together near a beam of sunlight in the barn. Jolene stood over a head taller than Elizabeth, who was small and petite. Jolene was tall for a girl and bigger boned. She was strong from years of hard work on their horse ranch, while Elizabeth preferred inside work.

Elizabeth pulled back, still sniffling, then managed a weak smile. "Guess we'd better go help Mama with supper."

Jolene nodded. "Let's go."

The two girls headed for the large ranch house, a breeze blowing their faded, but clean calico skirts.

Jolene looked at Elizabeth, who was walking with her head down. *At least she doesn't look Indian,* Jolene thought to herself. *That would only make it all the worse for teasing.*

Jolene herself clearly took after their Cheyenne mother. She had large, dark, almond-shaped eyes and dark hair that hung past her waist. Her nose was straight, and she walked with her shoulders back and her chin up. She was proud of her Indian blood, but sometimes it was hard.

Jolene was the only one of the seven children who really looked Indian. The others resembled their father, with light brown hair and blue-gray eyes.

The girls went up the steps and through the open door into the kitchen. Their mother had already started supper. She looked up as her daughters entered, a smile on her face. Pushing a strand of hair back off her forehead, she said cheerfully, "Just in time. I need someone to call your two older brothers in. They went fishing down to the creek."

"I'll go get them," Jolene said quickly, and started back out the door, bumping into her father. "Sorry, Pa."

He chuckled as she went on past.

As she went down the porch steps and turned toward the creek, she heard hoof beats.

Turning, she stopped and watched, her braid swinging, dust settling around her bare feet as a rider on a lathered horse pulled up in front of the house. She had no idea who it was.

Pa came out on the porch. "Howdy."

The man didn't dismount. Instead, he took off his hat and wiped his brow. "Howdy. Just came to warn ya," His voice was matter of fact. "There's a bunch of Johnny Rebs down at the depot in town. Just came in. We men are gettin' together a posse. We're gonna run 'em out."

Jolene felt as if her feet were rooted to the ground. Johnny Rebs? There'd been a war, but that was over.

Pa hadn't answered, but just stared at the man, sorrow in his eyes. "I was hopin' this kinda thing wouldn't happen. Guess it did."

The rider nodded. "S'pose you'll be comin' with us now. Any real man would want to help his town." His eyes were accusing as he looked down at Pa.

Pa met his gaze. "I'll think about it."

Jolene heard Mama gasp. "*Will—*"

Pa shushed her.

The man on the horse let his gaze sweep over the ranch. "Say, don't you have two boys who're old enough to be comin'?"

Pa's voice was calm, "They're only sixteen and seventeen."

"Thet's old enough."

"Not to my liking." Pa's voice was firm. "They won't be men until they're twenty-one. I ain't rushin' them."

The man looked down at Pa, and shifted a wad of tobacco in his mouth. He moved his tongue, about to spit. Ever so slightly, Pa moved his hand toward the Colt .45 tied at his thigh.

The man quickly spat over his shoulder, then sneered at Pa. "Well, injun lover, iffen they don' come, an' you don't come, we'll be after them and burn you out. Your town is gonna need you in a coupla days."

With that, he wheeled his horse and trotted out of the yard.

That night, as she lay in bed, Jolene heard voices coming from her parents' bedroom.

Slipping out of bed, Jolene walked barefoot to the door of the room that she shared with Elizabeth. Silently, she opened it. Going down the dark hallway and down the stairs, Jolene stopped beside the door to her parents' room. Her white nightgown swished around her ankles as she listened. She scarcely dared to breathe.

"Will, you can't go."

"Did you really think I would?" His voice grew softer. "The only reason I would go is if those Rebs started trouble."

Her mother's voice was trembling. "What about Pete and Jim? Will they go?"

"No. No, they'll stay here. I don't want them to have to face such things. Not yet."

"What if they want to go?"

"Then I can't stop them."

Jolene couldn't stand to listen any longer. Quietly, she went back up to her room and into her warm bed. Elizabeth stirred, but didn't waken.

What would happen if those Rebs started trouble?

Three days had passed since the man had come on horseback. As Jolene knelt by her bedside to say her prayers that night, she had an odd feeling.

Her prayers that night were longer than usual, and as she slipped into bed, she saw in the dim room, tears in Elizabeth's eyes. "Jolene," she whispered. "What if that man meant what he said about burning us out?"

So Jolene wasn't the only one who was scared.

Pulling the blankets up to her chin, Jolene reached out and took Elizabeth's hand, tears filling her own eyes. For a long time, the girls lay in silence. Then, finally, they both fell into a fitful sleep.

There was a slender crescent of a moon hanging in a pitch black sky. The ranch house was quiet and dark.

In the shadows beside the house, some figures moved. Voices.

"We'll burn them out. They don't want to fight the Rebs, we'll let them fight now. For their lives."

Another voice. "It's a good excuse to get the injuns out of town anyway. Never did like 'em."

Another voice. "By the time anyone finds out, we'll be oughta here, headin' out on the nearest train. Everyone'll think it was the Rebs."

There was the sound of tin cans, then someone held out a torch.

"Where's the kerosene?"

"Right here. Are all the shutters barred on the outside?"

"Good, guess we're ready."

Will smelled smoke. Opening his eyes, he looked around. It was dark. Too dark. He frowned. He hadn't barred the shutters last night.

Groping his way to the door, he opened it, only to be met by a wall of black smoke and orange flames.

"Fire!"

Ehaywee awoke to find flames creeping toward her bedside and Will clawing at the shutters. There was nothing to smash the shutters with. Will had already tried his pistol. It hadn't worked. When the door opened, flames had rolled in, despite the fact that Will had shut the door quickly. Flames spread. They were trapped.

Upstairs, Jim and Pete sprang out of bed and flung open the door. Running down the stairs, they both stopped and stared. All they could see before them was fire. Whirling, they tried to go back up the stairs, but within seconds, the flames had come around them. They, too, were trapped.

With wild eyes, Pete suddenly made a dash through the flames, toward the stairs. Screams of pain followed. Jim stared in disbelief at the flames that hid his brother.

The screams awoke Jolene. Smoke was coming under their bedroom door. Shaking Elizabeth awake, Jolene grabbed her and pulled her out of the bed.

"What?" Elizabeth was still half asleep.

Jolene didn't answer. Yanking open the door, she saw flames rolling up the stairs. There was no way to go anywhere. The stairs were between their room and everything else. Jolene slammed the door. There was no way to save anyone but themselves. But how? The window! They could climb out onto the roof!

Hurrying toward the window, Jolene began tugging on it. "Elizabeth, fill an pillowcase with everything you can fit."

Dazed, but hurrying, Elizabeth obeyed, shoving clothing into a emptied pillowcase.

Jolene climbed onto the roof, then reached a hand in to Elizabeth. Elizabeth clutched Jolene's hand tightly and clambered up beside her, the pillowcase clutched to her chest.

Out on the roof of the porch, a cool breeze blew. All was black except for the bit of light from the sliver of moon and orange glow from the fire. Jolene crawled to the edge of the roof and looked down. It was a ten-foot drop…but they had to jump. All around them, the orange flames lit the woods and barns with an eerie glow.

"We have to jump," Jolene said to Elizabeth. Elizabeth crouched on the roof, stricken with fear. "I'll go first," Jolene said. "And I can catch you." Elizabeth didn't answer.

Holding the edge of the roof, Jolene crouched. Swallowing her fear, she jumped. She landed in a crouching position on the ground. Down on the ground, she could feel the heat from the flames. The house could collapse any second. They had to get out of there.

Elizabeth was crouched at the edge of the roof. Jolene heard the sound of crying from inside the house. Sammie. There was no hope. Had anyone else gotten out? She could see flames licking at the upstairs windowsill. Fear went through her like a bolt of lightening. "Jump!" she screamed.

Elizabeth began to whimper, her face white with fear. "I can't!" she began to sob.

"You can! Jump!" Jolene's voice was hoarse.

Flames licked at the sill behind Elizabeth. Jolene began praying like she never had before. If her sister didn't jump, she would be burned to death by the orange flames.

Something crashed inside the house. Wood splintered.

CHAPTER TWO

Elizabeth jumped. She landed near Jolene, sprawled on her stomach Without a minute's hesitation, Jolene grabbed Elizabeth's hand and yanked her to her feet. Then, they took off running toward the barns. Behind them, the house cracked and splintered as the whole frame collapsed.

Jolene opened her eyes. Her back and neck ached and her left leg had fallen asleep. Where was she? Jolene looked around the barn. Elizabeth lay beside her, sprawled in the hay. They were in the hayloft. Then, Jolene remembered. The fire. The black smoke. The cries. Was the house still there?

Elizabeth stirred, then sat up and rubbed her eyes. She looked around with somber blue-gray eyes.

For a few minutes, the girls just sat in the soft hay, reminiscing in their minds, the night before. Jolene swallowed a lump in her throat. Never, had she felt so lost and alone as she did now. Her eyes fell on the pillowcase between them. What had Elizabeth managed to stuff into it?

Opening it, Jolene pulled out her everyday work dress and Elizabeth's school dress, two pairs of stockings and Jolene's moccasins. No shoes. She looked down at her sooty nightdress. Elizabeth was even worse.

"We might as well change," Jolene said, handing Elizabeth her school dress.

Wordlessly, Elizabeth took it.

After they had changed, Jolene headed for the ladder that led down from the hayloft. Once they were standing on the barn floor, Jolene realized there were no horses to be seen or heard. An unexpected stab of anger flashed through her. Who had done this and why?

"Jolene," Elizabeth's soft voice broke into her thoughts. "Do you think the man who told us about the Confederates has something to do with this?" Elizabeth refused to use the word "Rebs."

Jolene's dark eyes flashed in remembrance of his words. *"We'll burn you out."*

Her eyes met Elizabeth's blue-gray ones. Then she nodded.

Elizabeth's voice trembled and she was staring down at her bare feet. Morning sun shone in through the windows.

"Do you think anybody else got out of the house?"

Deep down inside, Jolene knew the answer, but she couldn't face it right now. She twisted her skirt in her hands. "Maybe. We could go look."

The girls went out of the open barn door and stopped. Jolene heard Elizabeth's quick intake of breath.

Before them, in a pile of blackened rubble and gray smoke, lay the remains of what had been home. The ground around it was hard-packed dirt, which had prevented the fire from spreading. There were hoof prints all over the ground from where someone had turned the horses loose.

Jolene closed her eyes as a cool morning breeze blew softly through her silky hair. This was all a nightmare. It had to be. When she opened her eyes, all would be well. But she knew that wouldn't happen.

She heard a broken sob behind her and opened her eyes just in time to see Elizabeth collapse on the dirt ground, sobbing. "It can't be true. It can't!" She raised pain-filled eyes to Jolene. "What are we going to do? Where will we live?"

Jolene felt a lump in her throat as she knelt down beside Elizabeth. She mustn't cry. For Elizabeth's sake, she must be strong. She soothed Elizabeth until the crying had stopped. "I don't know what we'll do," Jolene spoke quietly. "But we'll figure something out. Maybe…" Jolene thought fast. What *could* they do?

Standing up, Jolene pulled Elizabeth to her feet and dusted off her skirt. An idea was beginning to form. "We'll go to town," she said firmly. "Maybe I could get a job. We could stay in a boarding house." Taking a deep breath, Jolene went on, "We'll have to try to sell the ranch"

As much as it hurt, they didn't really have a choice. There was no way two young girls could manage a horse ranch on their own. *Especially without horses*, Jolene thought bitterly.

Elizabeth didn't answer, but just stood, staring at the pile of charred logs and ashes. The expression on her face made Jolene want to scream.

Then, Elizabeth looked at Jolene and nodded dully. "I suppose we don't have any other choice, do we."

It was more of a statement than a question. "I guess not." Jolene tried to sound strong, but inside she was quaking. Would it work? What was going to happen? They had nothing in terms of protection…or did they? Feeling her waistband, Jolene's heart leaped. In a small pouch, tucked out of sight was a knife. She must have forgotten to take it out the night before. Well, at least it was something.

Just then, Jolene heard something. Whirling around, she looked toward the corner of the barn. Esperanza! The buckskin filly was coming toward them. She lowered her head when she reached the girls, and Jolene put out a hand. The filly nuzzled it softly, lipping her fingers in search for food.

Elizabeth reached out to stroke the filly's neck and Jolene saw she was glad to see the horse.

Pa had bought the horse from a Mexican, two years ago for Jolene's twelfth birthday. Jolene had broken her and trained her so she was gentle as a lamb. And whenever the filly had managed to get loose, she had always returned. "I guess we won't be walking to town," Jolene said softly. Elizabeth nodded.

Jolene's stomach rumbled with hunger. Food! That was another problem. If only they had a gun, she could shoot a deer. Suddenly , she remembered something. Pa had a twelve gauge shotgun with two boxes of shells in the barn. They had been for Pete's birthday.

"Come on," Jolene said to Elizabeth, grabbing Esperanza's mane. She led the horse into the barn. "Saddle her and bridle her," Jolene told the confused Elizabeth and quickly went to the very end stall. It wasn't being used, so there was no straw on the floor.

Kneeling, Jolene slipped two fingers into a cracked floorboard and pulled up hard. The board came up, revealing the gleaming shotgun and the boxes of shells. Stuffing the ammo into the pouch at her waist, Jolene felt thankful for all the times her father had spent teaching her to shoot and handle guns. She had hunted with him and could shoot as well or better than her brothers.

Jolene suddenly felt like bursting into tears. The metal on the shotgun seemed very cold. Never again would her father or any of her brothers handle a gun again.

"Why?" she whispered as a breeze blew through the open windows. "Why did this have to happen to my family?" She felt angry, then ashamed. "I guess God had His reasons for taking them. Thank You for at least sparing the two of us." She swiped at a hot tear that trickled down her cheek. "Please, help us."

Then, she quickly headed back to her sister, the shotgun cold and heavy against her palms.

Esperanza was saddled and bridled. Elizabeth was standing beside the horse, her face red and swollen from crying. Her eyes widened as she caught sight of the shotgun. Her eyes widened even more when she saw the look of determination on Jolene's face.

Jolene carefully slipped the shotgun into the scabbard that hung from the saddle. "Let's go," she said to Elizabeth. "Do you want to ride front or back?"

"Back. You can handle horses better than I can."

Jolene knew it was true. When she rode, with or without a saddle, she felt at one with the horse. While Elizabeth sat inside sewing, Jolene had worked alongside her father and brothers. Jolene could sew and cook, but had never loved to do them as Elizabeth had. Elizabeth had been the lady.

The girls' manners were totally different also. Elizabeth was more dramatic, tending to get queasy around blood, and she'd always loved new clothes. She was sweet and friendly, and everyone liked her. She was pretty too, though she didn't seem to know it.

Jolene was quieter, and liked to think. She was a hard worker when she was needed, and she loved to hunt. She was strong for a girl and a bit shy around people. She liked to draw and read. And Jolene thought of herself as plain—especially compared to her sister.

"As different as black and white," Pa used to say.

Jolene broke away from her thoughts and swung into the saddle easily. Elizabeth took her offered hand and managed to swing up behind her, and arranged her skirts. "Do you have the pillowcase?"

"Yes."

They rode out of the barn and into the yard. There was no longer smoke rising from the rubble. Jolene felt tears sting her eyes. Would they ever come back? She had a feeling they wouldn't. If only those Rebs had never come to town, her family would be alive.

Please, God, help us to get through these hard times, Jolene prayed silently. Then, she kicked Esperanza with her heels, sending little puffs of dust up from the horse's coat.

They took off at a trot, out of the yard, down the road, away from the only home they had ever known. Broken Arrow Ranch. It should have been named Broken Heart Ranch. Jolene knew better than to look back. If she did, she would burst into tears. Already she felt Elizabeth shaking with quiet sobs.

They had to be strong, or they too, would die. Of starvation. Or pneumonia. Or grief.

CHAPTER THREE

The town was set back against a mountain, surrounded by pine and aspen. It was a rather small town, with a lot of people, most of whom were related.

Jolene felt people staring at the two of them as they rode toward the small bank. The stares weren't unfriendly, just curious, but Jolene felt her scalp prickle. She had never really associated with the town's people before and had no idea what they were like.

The girls dismounted in front of the small, but sturdily built bank at the end of the street. As Jolene tied the horse to the hitching rail, she noticed Elizabeth smoothing her skirts and patting her hair. Jolene quickly tried to smooth her rumpled skirt. She knew they must have looked a sight: two girls without shoes riding double on a horse, with a shotgun stuck in the scabbard of the saddle.

Jolene managed a smile at an elderly couple who were passing by, and got a smile and a nod in return.

Lifting her chin, Jolene headed for the bank. If Pa had money, they would need it. Elizabeth was right behind her as she opened the door and stepped inside. Before them was a mousy-looking man in a green eye shade, standing behind what looked like wooden bars. Jolene had never been in a bank before, but she swallowed her fear and walked up to the wooden bars.

The man looked up with a wan smile. "Can I help you?"

"I would like to withdraw some money." Jolene hoped that was what you were supposed to say.

"Certainly. How much would you like to , uh, withdraw, and, uh, what's your name?"

"My name's Jolene Culhaine and this is my sister Elizabeth." Jolene felt uncertain. "How much money do we have in the bank?"

"Uh, well," the man began.

Then a door opened from behind him, and another man stepped out, light glinting off a gold chain looped on his vest. He wore a stiff, pressed black suit that looked rather odd in his rugged surroundings. He had a pale complexion and was thin.

He looked at the two girls. "Pardon me, but I couldn't help overhearing your conversation. You girls don't sound familiar."

Jolene nodded. "My father was William Culhaine. He had an account here."

"How am I to believe you?" The man was smiling through long, thin lips.

"You have to."

The man's smile seemed to freeze. "I do, do I? I own the bank here and I don't go around handing money out to strangers. Especially young girls."

Jolene straightened and looked him in the eye. "Our ranch was burned to the ground last night and my Pa is no longer alive to take care of anything."

The man shook his head. "Now, now girls. I'm sorry to hear that, but we just can't go giving money out to just anyone."

Jolene glared at him. "It's our money."

The man shook his head. "I'm sorry girls. No." He turned on his heel and went back into his room.

The girls rode out of town with a sense of defeat. They had no money and no one wanted work. There was no place to go. The girls were riding out of town, the opposite way they had come in. Hopefully, there was another town within a few days' ride.

For the next two days, the girls followed the road, eating a few early berries and greens. Jolene managed to shoot a rabbit and a few squirrels, and they drank water from nearby streams.

The third day of riding, Jolene saw smoke rising above a cluster of cottonwoods about a mile ahead. She felt wary. It was a campfire, she knew that much. But what kind of people were there?

It was late afternoon. Jolene knew Elizabeth was getting exhausted and, despite herself, her own stomach growled.

"I think we should go see who that is," Elizabeth said as they rounded a curve.

"I don't know." Jolene had an uneasy feeling. "Maybe we should just mind our own business."

"Oh, come on Jolene! We wouldn't bother anyone. Just see who it is— maybe they could tell us where the nearest town is."

Jolene felt herself giving in. Maybe they should. "Alright." Jolene turned the horse in the direction of the slender wisp of smoke that they could now smell. It was worth a try. Nothing bad could happen…could it?

They moved farther off the road and deeper into the stand of cottonwood. It was quiet except for the soft thud of Esperanza's hooves and the soft rustle of leaves and branches against their clothes. There seemed to be no birds, no squirrels, no nothing. But the smell of the campfire was very near.

It should be just through these trees, Jolene thought, some of her uneasiness returning.

It was. As they cleared the clump of trees, a campfire came into sight in the middle of a small clearing. But there was no sign of anyone. Jolene reined in Esperanza and studied the surroundings. The fire was small, but was burning brightly. Hanging between two spliced sticks, was a coffee pot. And it smelled like a full one. There were three bedrolls scattered throughout the camp. There were boot prints and hoof prints in the dirt.

"There's no one here."

Jolene heard the disappointment in her sister's voice. "We should probably just move on." Jolene couldn't shake off that odd feeling. Something was not right.

"Oh, couldn't we just wait a little?" Elizabeth pleaded. "Maybe they have food. You know we're both hungry." Without waiting for an answer, Elizabeth grasped her skirts and slid to the ground. Jolene had no choice but to follow.

Holding Esperanza's reins, Jolene watched warily as her sister went over to the fire. In the cool spring breeze, the fire must have felt wonderfully warm.

Jolene felt a sudden stab of jealousy as she studied her sister. Around Elizabeth, she felt very plain and tom-boyish in comparison. Sometimes Jolene wished she could be more like her younger sister. Then Jolene pushed the thoughts aside. She was who she was, and she wasn't going to change. Not for anything.

Elizabeth turned to come back to Jolene. Something moved behind her. Jolene stiffened when she saw the movement.

A man burst out of the bushes and ran straight for Elizabeth.

"Run!" Jolene screamed. She felt as if she were in slow motion as she reached up for the shotgun.

Elizabeth looked back over her shoulder and screamed. Picking up her skirts, she ran. She only got a few steps before she tripped over a stick and fell.

Then, just as Jolene whipped the shotgun to her shoulder, she felt someone clamp a strong hand over her mouth and nose. Unable to breathe, she let the shotgun fall to the ground, and clawed at the hand over her face. The man let go and grabbed her wrists, twisting them behind her back until she cried out in pain.

The other man had his arms around Elizabeth, pinning her arms to her sides.

Both men had scruffy hair and had on worn and dirty clothes. They both looked young. The one mid-twenties and the other younger yet.

Jolene had stopped struggling for a moment to see if Elizabeth was alright. The fear and anger in her sister's eyes gave Jolene a sudden burst of fury and energy. With one quick yank, she twisted her wrists free and swung her fist at the man who had been holding her. It hit him solidly in the mouth. For a split second, the man stared at her in shock. Then, he spit blood onto the ground and lunged for her.

Jolene dodged, almost tripping over her long skirts, and snatched up the shotgun from the ground. Leveling it at the man, who now froze in lunging position, she moved so both men were in front of her and within shooting range, then motioned for the one to release Elizabeth. "What do you men want with us?" she tried to keep the fear from her voice.

"What were you doing snooping around our camp?" the man in front of her snarled. Muttering under his breath, he spat blood again.

Suddenly, Jolene heard another sound behind her and before she could turn, she felt something hard hit her head.

The last thing she remembered was Elizabeth's scream. Then, blackness.

CHAPTER FOUR

Jolene awoke to a dull throb at the back of her head. The sun was slowly sinking out of sight behind a mountain. Jolene sat up and the throb became worse. Where was she and what was she doing on the ground? Suddenly, she remembered. The men! Looking around, she saw no one. Esperanza was gone. And worst of all, Jolene realized with a sinking feeling, that Elizabeth was gone also.

There was only a small spark of gladness when Jolene realized they had left the shotgun. When she had fallen, her skirts had covered it completely. For once, she was glad she had such long full skirts.

But how was she to find Elizabeth? Standing, Jolene straightened her skirts and pushed back her long dark hair, which had somehow come loose from its string. She couldn't very well go after the two men. No, make that three. Someone had hit her over the head. And she had seen the men wearing guns.

Suddenly, Jolene straightened her shoulders with determination. Somehow, she would have to track them down and try to help Elizabeth escape. Somehow.

It was the third day of hard walking and exhaustion when Jolene lost the trail. She had followed it easily the first day, but then it had gotten harder.

She knew she was far behind, but she couldn't give up. She tried not to think of what they could do to her sweet little sister.

Jolene had eaten very little in the past few days and she knew she couldn't last much longer. Her stomach felt hollow. Her clothes hung on her now thin frame. But she wouldn't let up. She hadn't helped her sister escape from their burning house just to let her be taken away by some scruffy men. She felt both indignation and anger.

She couldn't, wouldn't let up. Until now. The trail seemed to stop with no more sign of horses or people.

After a few hours of circling, searching for anything that would represent a trail, Jolene felt close to tears. Nothing. Somehow, they had covered their back trail. Either that, or it had just gotten old.

Once again, the sun was beginning to set. Jolene felt lost, hungry, and desperate. There was nothing she could think of to do but push forward. She started off, trudging through a meadow filled with violets.

That night, Jolene curled up under a large hemlock. Before going to sleep, Jolene sent up a quick prayer to God, asking Him to help her through everything and find Elizabeth. And wherever Elizabeth was, to keep her safe.

Jolene awoke the next morning to the smell of woodsmoke. She kept her eyes closed as fear sent cold chills up her spine. Someone was moving around. Then she smelled coffee and bacon. A coffee pot rattled. Someone started to whistle a slow tune.

Cautiously, Jolene opened her eyes. Someone had covered her with a blanket.

A man in a broad-brimmed gray hat crouched by the fire. He wore dusty clothes and there was an Appaloosa tied to a tree a few feet away.

Jolene felt for her shotgun, but her fingers closed around pine needles. He had taken the shotgun! Well, she still had her knife.

Unexpectedly, her stomach growled—loudly. The man looked up and saw her looking at him. He was in his mid fifties, with a fringe of gray hair sticking out from underneath his hat. There was a growth of stubble on his chin. "So, ye're awake, are ye, lass?" He spoke with a thick Irish brogue.

Jolene glared at him. It was quite obvious that she was awake! Whoever heard of someone sleeping with their eyes open?

The man smiled in return to her glare, and casually poured himself a cup of coffee, steam rising from the brown liquid.

Jolene's stomach growled again.

He grinned at her. "Ye'd best get over here, lass, and have a bite to eat. I kin tell ye're hungry."

Reluctantly, Jolene stood up and shook out her rumpled skirts. Her back felt stiff and her legs cramped. Pushing her loose hair back from her face, Jolene accepted the cup of coffee the man held out to her. Warily, she watched him as he began flipping bacon. Could he be one of the men who had captured Elizabeth? The man seemed to sense her hostility.

"Don't worry, lass, I'm not going to bite ye." He handed her a tin plate of food. "My name's Danny O'Grady. Come from Californ-y where I been lookin' fer gold. Found nuthin an' decided to look a bit farther east. Liked the

looks o' the Colorado territory an' thought I could find me a job."
He looked at her, curiosity showing plainly in his blue eyes. "An' where are ye from, lass? Ye look like ye'd be lonesome travelin' by yerself."

Jolene began to relax at his open honesty. And the food tasted wonderful. "I'm Jolene Culhaine. I came from a horse ranch. Over that way, I think." She pointed east.

"Came?"

"It burned down."

"Burned?" His brow furrowed and he paused to take a sip of his coffee. "How?"

Jolene swallowed a bite of food before she answered. Tears blurred her eyes at the memory of that night. The next thing she knew, she had told the man the whole story, starting with the man who had come to ask Pa to help get rid of the Confederates.

The Irishman listened intently while she finished talking. "I know how ye feel lass. I lost my own wee lad an' wife a year ago in Californ-y. Didn't even get to see them. When I got the letter in the gold fields sayin' they had died, I jest lit out. I was grief stricken."

For a few minutes, they sat in silence, each deep in their own thoughts. Jolene began remembering her siblings, one by one.

First, there was Jim. He had been seventeen. He had been the bold one of her two older brothers. He had been handsome and rather reckless, but had done his share of the work. He'd had a liking for trout fishing. When he wasn't courting Sarah Lynn, the girl who lived down the road, he could usually be found by the stream behind the house, hauling trout out one by one. Sarah had moved though, just last year. Jim had been angry.

Well, he won't be anymore, Jolene thought sadly.

Pete, too had liked fishing. Maybe more than Jim had. Pete had been sixteen. More withdrawn than Jim, he was a hard worker and usually willing to help others. The surprising thing about him was his sense of humor. Most people didn't think he would be one to tell jokes and play pranks, but he had been. When Jolene and Pete were younger, they had always ganged up on Jim, and nearly driven him crazy with their teasing.

Then there had been Davie. He'd been eleven. Just old enough to start hunting. He'd been so proud when he'd killed his first deer. He'd been one to forget his chores and start building something out of string and kindling. Once, he'd built a mouse trap. It had worked better than the ones in town.

Then came Martha, who had been nine. She'd been rather bossy and determined. She seemed always to be struggling with one task or another, always trying to do it better than Elizabeth or Jolene. But she had been the affectionate one, always willing to give a hug.

Then Sammie. The youngest at six. Mama's baby. Everyone's pet. He'd been a bit spoiled, but was sweet and always tried to help out. Jolene shuddered as she remembered his cries from the burning room. They would always haunt her, above everything else. Her baby brother she hadn't been able to help.

Quickly, Jolene pushed the accusing thoughts away.

There was Elizabeth. Though two years apart, they had always been best friends, always sharing everything.

Was Elizabeth dead too?

O'Grady's voice broke into her thoughts. "How long ago since ye lost their trail, lass?"

Jolene's heart skipped a beat, then she hesitated. "A day."

"Headin' which way?"

"West." Jolene wondered why he was asking all the questions.

He rose to his feet. "Come, lass. We're going to find your sister."

Jolene stared up at him, speechless.

"You don't think they killed her, do ye?"

"No," Jolene said slowly. "But why…"

"Because I know how ye feel, lass, an' I just can't walk off an' leave ye hare alone. Mebbe with God's help we kin find yer sister."

CHAPTER FIVE

They rode double, despite Jolene's reluctance. They could move faster if they both rode. Jolene's leg rubbed against her shotgun, which was stuck in a scabbard on the right side of the horse. She knew O'Grady must trust her, leaving her easily within range of grasping the shotgun. Jolene still wasn't sure if she could trust this man. He seemed honest enough. And at least he was helping her find Elizabeth. Or at least she hoped he was helping her.

They rode in silence for hours, not stopping. The sun beat down unmercifully and Jolene ached from sitting in the saddle. Her stomach growled loudly and her lips were dry in want for water.

When she thought she could stand it no longer, she caught sight of a building through a grove of beech just ahead.

"There's a town," O'Grady said.

A town? Could the men who kidnapped Elizabeth have gone to town? It was likely that they could have.

If O'Grady hadn't come along, I wouldn't have stood a chance of finding my sister, Jolene thought. The kidnappers could have easily made up a story and stayed in town for one night, and be gone before Jolene had reached town.

They're probably gone by now if they were in town, Jolene thought, but still her heartbeat quickened. They could be so close to finding her sister!

The town was small and not overly busy. Like Jolene's hometown, it was set back against a mountain, surrounded by cottonwood and pine.

O'Grady and Jolene dismounted at a hitching rail and O'Grady tied the horse. "We'd best ask around about yer sister first," he said to Jolene. "There's a good chance they stopped here, an' if they did, someone might know where they are or where they went." He glanced around. "Ye'd best stay here by me horse an' keep a look out."

He started off down the boardwalk and for the first time, Jolene realized he limped. She wondered if he'd fought in the war.

The war. It seemed like such a long time ago. Her father had fought in the war. He'd never talked about it, and Jolene had known he was trying to forget it. The territory of Colorado had fought for the Union, for freedom of the slaves.

Jolene stroked the horse's neck. What would it be like to live down South, she wondered. Were all the people as cruel as she had heard? Did *everyone* own slaves? What about the people who moved from the North? Did they change their minds about slavery? Jolene began wishing for some answers. Pa had never told her anything, and she didn't know whether or not to believe what was read in the papers.

Jolene sighed and studied the town around her. There were a group of young girls, giggling and talking together in front of a millinery shop. A little boy, a big mutt beside him, lay sprawled under a tree near the general store. Everyone seemed content and happy. It didn't seem like anything could go wrong in this little town.

There was O'Grady limping back to her from the sheriff's office. Jolene couldn't read the expression on his face. He stopped beside her, a little short of breath, and took off his hat, slapping it against his leg. His hair was completely gray. "They were here, lass. Might even still be."

Jolene's heart sped up. Could Elizabeth be so close? "Are…are we going to look for them?"

"Of course! We didn't come all this way just for nothing now, did we, lass?"

Jolene shook her head.

"The sheriff said it'd be best if we tried the hotel first. They stayed there last night."

They made their way to the tall building with the sign Dingham's Hotel on the outside, and entered. There was a young woman behind the counter. She looked up as they came in. "Can I help you?" She had a pleasant face, with a voice to match.

"Yes, ma'am." O'Grady removed his hat. "We're lookin' fer three men who come in here last night with a young girl. She was about twelve." O'Grady looked inquiringly at Jolene, who nodded. "She was kidnapped a few days ago."

The young woman looked horrified. "I don't think they were in here. What did the girl look like?"

"She had light brown hair," Jolene said softly, "And blue-gray eyes. She was wearing a blue calico dress and she didn't have shoes."

The woman pursed her lips. "Last night two young men came in here with a young woman and a girl just like the one you described." She paused. "They left the girl behind."

Jolene's heart gave one hard thump and then seemed to stop. Dead? She dared not voice her thoughts.

"Where is she?" O'Grady's voice sounded gravelly.

"Room twenty-three. Up the stairs, fourth one on the left. Here's the key." She handed it to O'Grady, who took it solemnly.

"Thank you, ma'am. Much obliged."

They went up the polished mahogany steps, O'Grady's boots making echoing sounds on the hard wood.

"Fourth one on the left," O'Grady muttered, "Room twenty-three." He looked at the numbers on the doors.

Jolene felt as if someone was squeezing the breath out of her, as he put the key in the slot and turned it. The door opened under his grasp and Jolene took a deep breath as he peered in, then he looked at Jolene, a frown on his face. "Nobody's in there."

Nobody...Jolene couldn't believe it. "There has to be."

He stepped into the room and glanced around, then froze. Standing in the far corner of the room, was a young girl with a white face and a derringer trained directly at him. O'Grady then made the mistake of taking a step backwards. "Eliz—"

Elizabeth closed her eyes and squeezed the trigger. The little gun went off. O'Grady stumbled backwards, and Jolene stifled a scream, as the bullet buried itself in the wood, not inches from her head.

Then, there was dead silence as Elizabeth stared at O'Grady, who was backed against the open door. Jolene cautiously moved around him and into the room. "It's a good thing you're still a bad shot, Elizabeth, or you would have killed a very nice person."

With a cry, Elizabeth dropped the derringer and flew into her sister's arms.

The three of them sat at a small table across the street from the hotel. O'Grady had recovered from his minor shock and his face was no longer a sickly white. In fact, he seemed to enjoy the fact that Elizabeth was alive. Elizabeth, too had recovered, and was chattering a mile a minute. "After the woman hit Jolene, they grabbed me and took off. After a while, the one man wanted to know if I was hurt. I said no. Then he asked where I was headed and why I was traveling with a redskin. I told him I was traveling to nowhere and 'that redskin' was my sister. It took a while for them to believe it and then they said they were sorry. They thought you were dangerous and they should rescue me."

"I was dangerous," Jolene said dryly, "until I got hit on the head by that lady."

Elizabeth giggled. "They were all on their way to Kansas to visit some relatives. There were two brothers and a sister. They were actually really nice," she said thoughtfully. "After they found out what had happened to us. And since they didn't want to lose time finding you—or risking getting shot—I told them you still had the shotgun—they decided to leave me in town where I could maybe get help. They paid board in the hotel for three days and my money for food." Elizabeth handed a small money pouch to Jolene. "I'm sure we can use it."

"They left you a gun too," O'Grady said matter-of-factly.

"Yes," Elizabeth's eyes gleamed. "That was in case some dangerous man broke into my room."

O'Grady chuckled, "I still feel sorry for the poor lady who gave us the key. I wonder if she ever got her hair smoothed back down after hearing the shot."

CHAPTER SIX

The girls decided to stay the night in Elizabeth's hotel room and O'Grady would stay in one down the hall. Jolene knew, now that he had helped her find Elizabeth, he would want to get rid of them, though he didn't say anything.

As she lay beside Elizabeth in the dark hotel room, she herself wondered what they would do. She felt Elizabeth roll over beside her and heard a soft voice, "Are you awake, Jolene?"

"Mm-hmm."

Elizabeth propped herself up on her elbows. "I can't sleep."

"What are you thinking about?"

Usually, Elizabeth had no trouble getting to sleep. "Those people…the ones who thought they were rescuing me." She paused a minute to make sure Jolene was listening, then continued softly. "The lady's name was Eulalia. She was probably twenty. She was the middle sibling. She's engaged to someone in Kansas and hasn't seen him since the war's over. She forced her brothers to bring her with them."

Jolene began to get drowsy, but forced herself to stay awake.

"The one young man was twenty-one, I think. His name was Joel. He was the one who caught you." Elizabeth rolled so her back was to Jolene. "The other man was Ben. His full name is Benjamin Joseph Wheatstalk."

Jolene caught a different note in Elizabeth's tone as she spoke of Ben, and suddenly, she felt wide awake.

Elizabeth continued. "He's just a boy really—seventeen. He's different from Joel somehow." She hesitated, "I mean Joel's really nice, but…" her voice trailed off.

"You like Ben better," Jolene finished, beginning to realized Elizabeth was no longer a little girl.

"Mm-hmm."

Then there was silence. Lying in the dark room, Jolene pondered over her sister's words. Could she—maybe—like Ben as more than a friend?

But she was only twelve. Almost thirteen. Jolene wasn't sure what to think. Elizabeth was growing up fast.

One thing Jolene did know was that she was glad Ben hadn't stayed in town.

The two girls stood in front of the livery stable from where they had retrieved Esperanza. Ben had left her there for Elizabeth. O'Grady was, with some reluctance, getting ready to go on his own way. He mounted his horse and looked down at the two girls. "I feel kinda bad, leavin' two young lassies like yerselves."

"You started out to go someplace and we aren't going to hold you back," Jolene said quietly. "We'll be fine."

"Well then, I'll be off. Remember, I'll always come if ye need me."

He kicked the horse into a trot. Jolene felt a sense of uneasiness as she watched him go. Had they done the right thing, not going with him?

"I feel as if my last hope just vanished," Elizabeth said softly.

Jolene looked at her sister and made up her mind. "I think we'll stay in town a few days before we head out. Maybe we could find a job here. Then we wouldn't have to leave."

They did get jobs, Elizabeth as a cleaning girl at the hotel, and Jolene as a serving girl. They worked cheap, but they got a free room and free meals too. That was more than enough.

At bedtime, the girls usually talked of their family and the life they'd had before the fire. To Jolene, the conversations helped to ease the pain of loss.

Then, one day, while Jolene and Elizabeth were taking an afternoon break, a middle-aged woman with a little boy of about six, walked into the hotel. She carried a bundle in her arms and she looked weary. Jolene ceased her talking with Elizabeth and looked at the little boy. He looked oddly like someone she knew. He had flaming hair and sharp blue eyes in a thin freckled face.

His mother's hair was streaked with gray and her forehead was criss-crossed with lines of worry and age.

The two went up to the main desk where young woman, Miss Johnson, handled the rooms.

"Hello, miss. Do ye have a room ye could spare for me an' me lad?"

She was Irish, that much, Jolene could discern.

"Yes, of course," Miss Johnson said, smiling at the little boy. "What's your name?" She took out a sheet of paper with the names of the people who came and went.

"Meagan O'Grady," the woman answered. "An' this is me son, Sean."

O'Grady! Elizabeth and Jolene stared at each other. Danny O'Grady had told them he had lost his wife and son a year ago while he was away panning for gold. Could this woman be a relation?

"Elizabeth," Miss Johnson called. "Will you show Mrs. O'Grady to room number seventeen? And give her a list of the hotel rules, will you please?"

Elizabeth and Jolene stood up from the bottom of the staircase where they had been sitting, and led Mrs. O'Grady up the stairs to her room. Jolene could see Elizabeth was bubbling with curiosity about the woman as she opened the door to room seventeen.

Once inside, the woman set down her bundle on the bed. "Thank you, girls."

As they were about to leave, Elizabeth suddenly turned back. "Ma'am, we couldn't help overhearing that your name is O'Grady. Do you know a Daniel O'Grady?"

The woman paled. "No, I don't think…what does he look like?"

"He's of medium height," Jolene broke in, "With blue eyes like your son's and gray hair."

"And he limps," Elizabeth finished.

The woman looked even paler. "Which leg? His left?"

"How did you know?" Elizabeth was surprised.

"Because." The woman took a deep breath. "He's my husband."

"How.." Jolene began.

"Come an' sit," the woman said, "an' I'll tell ye." She glanced at her son, who had been standing beside her the whole time. "What's your names, girls?"

"Jolene."

"Elizabeth."

"Well," the woman began, "last year me husband Danny went to Californ-y to pan fer gold. We—Sean and I—lived in Missouri when we got a letter. When I read it, it said Danny had died two weeks ago, of scurvy, and was already buried." Mrs. O'Grady took another deep breath as if to calm herself. "Fer a while we stayed put. Then we decided to move to Colorado. We didn't have much money but we had two horses and a wagon. And here we are."

They were all silent a moment before she spoke softly. "I never got proof that he was dead. All through those long months I never really felt he was dead. I was always expecting him to come home."

Again, they were silent, watching sunlight play on the smooth floorboards.

"There's no doubt he's your husband," Jolene said finally. "Three days ago, after helping me find Elizabeth, he rode out of this town. If you wanted, we could help you find him again."

"Would you?" Mrs. O'Grady's eyes shone. "Oh, I would be forever indebted to you if we could only find him." She turned to Sean. "What do ye think, Sean?"

His blue eyes, so like his father's were hopeful. "I think we should try to find Da."

"Then it's settled." Mrs. O'Grady turned back to the two girls. "Tomorrow we could go in the wagon if ye are willin'."

"We'll go tomorrow," Jolene said firmly. "We'll tell Miss Johnson that we won't be workin' for her any longer."

"Oh," Mrs. O'Grady looked troubled. "I couldn't ask you to quit yer jobs."

"You're not," Jolene assured her. "We want to."

"We know what it's like to lose your family," Elizabeth said softly, "and we're indebted to Mr. O'Grady. We'll help you find him if it's the last thing we do."

CHAPTER SEVEN

*F*ollow *your heart. Let it tell you what to do and where to go.* Pa's words ran through Jolene's head as the wagon rumbled out of town. Mrs. O'Grady was driving the team of bays. Esperanza was tied behind the wagon. Jolene and Elizabeth sat beside Mrs. O'Grady on the hard wagon seat. Sean lay among the bundles in the back of the wagon, gazing up at the blue sky.

Jolene wondered if they were doing the right thing. The whole situation seemed rather strange. Who had sent the letters to the O'Gradys saying their spouses were dead? It was just all too confusing.

They traveled in the direction Jolene and Elizabeth had seen Daniel O'Grady ride off. The day was warming up quickly and the April air was still. They were all silent as they rode onward, bouncing on the wooden wagon seat.

Then, about high noon, they rounded a curve in the road and saw a bundle and a book on the side of the road. Mrs. O'Grady pulled the horses to a stop. "We may as well stop fer a bite to eat. Lena, would ye see what that bundle is?"

Jolene hopped down from the wagon and just stood for a minute, letting her legs get the feeling of standing after sitting so long. Elizabeth slid down behind her, nearly knocking her over.

Jolene quickly moved out of her way and walked over to the book and bundle laying on the ground a few yards away from each other. The flour sack had something in it, and Jolene could see that the book was a Bible. Jolene picked up the Bible and gently dusted it off. It looked just like the one Pa had always carried in his saddlebags when he was away for a day or so. She opened the front cover to look for a name. Written in an elegant script were the words, "To my husband Daniel O'Grady, with Love, Meagan O'Grady."

Jolene caught her breath. Mr. O'Grady must have dropped it…but how? Jolene heard Mrs. O'Grady call for her to come eat. Elizabeth had helped to lay out the food under a tree a few yards away. Jolene quickly switched the

Bible to her other hand, and stooped to pick up the sack. Then, she realized both her hand and the back of the Bible were covered with sticky blood.

Picking up the sack, Jolene turned and hurried over to the trio awaiting her. "Look!" she held out the Bible. "It's Mr. O'Grady's and it has blood on it!"

Mrs. O'Grady turned three shades paler than she normally was and took the book with trembling fingers. "I gave him this the year we were married."

"What's in the sack?" Elizabeth asked eagerly.

"I don't know." Jolene opened it and the two girls peered inside. "Clothes!" they said in unison. They looked at Mrs. O'Grady again, who was staring at the Bible.

"What could have happened?" Elizabeth whispered.

Jolene shivered and glanced around. She half expected someone to leap out of the bushes at them. "I'll look around," she said, handing Elizabeth the sack.

Going over to the grassy patch where the Bible and sack had lain, she examined the ground. Nothing except for some blood and…hoof prints! They appeared to be coming out of nowhere, but at least they were something to follow.

Jolene hurried over to the O'Gradys and Elizabeth. "There's prints where his horse walked. They're still a little fresh. If we hurry—"

"Let's go." Mrs. O'Grady was gathering up the food and blanket. "We can at least try."

Then, they were back in the wagon and following the tracks slowly along the road, Jolene keeping a careful eye around them. She made sure the shotgun was close at hand. She had no idea what could happen and she wasn't going to take any chances.

The sun was sinking low behind the hills as the wagon rolled to a stop under a large cottonwood. They all ached from riding in the wagon and, now in the semi-darkness, they were all a bit jumpy.

Elizabeth and Jolene helped Mrs. O'Grady get out jerky, hardtack, and canteens of water. Jolene built a fire while Sean scrambled to find some larger sticks. No one was hungry that night, but they forced themselves to eat. Mrs. O'Grady was especially quiet, and sat for a long time watching the flames of the fire, until Sean laid his head in her lap and closed his eyes.

Then, she rose, her shadow long and dark, the flames casting an eerie glow over them all. It brought to Jolene's memory the awful night of the fire that burned down their house.

"It's time to get to bed," Mrs. O'Grady said firmly. "We need to rest if we're to get up in the mornin'."

Jolene and Elizabeth helped spread out blankets to make two beds—one for Mrs. O'Grady and Sean, and the other for Elizabeth and Jolene.

The night was cool and a breeze blew down from the tree tops. Clouds covered the full moon. The two girls slid under the blankets. Jolene knew Elizabeth was afraid. She could feel her trembling. Jolene, too, felt uneasy. A coyote howled and, involuntarily, Jolene shivered. Sean whimpered and Jolene heard Mrs. O'Grady comforting him with soft words. The fire had almost gone out.

Jolene watched the glowing coals, and realized the fire should be kept going. If any animal came, it would be frightened off by the flames. Jolene crawled out of the blankets and quickly began rebuilding the fire.

Green-yellow eyes suddenly glowed at the edge of the camp, then disappeared. Jolene felt tense, as if waiting for something to happen. Fear sliced through her as a twig snapped.

Help me, please, she prayed silently as she crawled back in beside Elizabeth.

Then, it seemed as if everything broke loose at once. A log in the fire suddenly snapped, sending bright flames shooting high, sparks crackling. Something, seemingly huge, crashed through the brush. A black shadow suddenly appeared a few feet from Jolene and Elizabeth.

All four people in the little camp lay, paralyzed for a split second. Then, both Elizabeth and Sean screamed.

CHAPTER EIGHT

Jolene's fingers closed around the cold barrel of the shotgun as the shadow came forward. It was a man, his hands held in the air. "I didn't mean to startle all of ya so."

"Ben!" Elizabeth sat bolt upright. "What are you doing here?"

Ben looked down at the two girls. Elizabeth's bright face was illuminated by the bright flames and her hair cascaded in a tangled array down her back. Her blue-gray eyes were sparkling with excitement.

Then, he looked at Jolene. Her dark features were shadowed by darkness, her hair also cascading down her back, shining in the firelight. Her eyes seemed to glitter with wariness and he could see her one hand tightly gripping a shotgun partially hidden by blankets. She looked pretty, but she also looked like she would shoot him if he didn't speak up.

"I see you found your sister," he said gravely, his eyes on Elizabeth. "Will she shoot me if I move?"

"I'll shoot only if you need it," came Jolene's cool reply.

Ben nodded and relaxed. "I don't need it."

The tension seemed to break, and the two girls and Mrs. O'Grady stood up, shaking out their skirts.

"What are you doing here, Ben?" Elizabeth repeated her question. "I thought you were on your way to Kansas."

Ben kept an eye on Jolene's shotgun. "We were. But we all started feeling pretty bad about taking you from your sister and leaving you alone in town, so when we were about a days ride away, we turned back. Eulalia wanted to make sure you found your sister."

"What took you so long?" Jolene asked, eyeing the thin young man in front of her. He wore the common cattle rancher's hat and Levis. The hair she could see from under his hat was sandy colored. So this was Ben.

"Well, we came upon an Irishman by the name of O'Grady—"

"Danny!" Mrs. O'Grady gasped.

"He said he knew you girls and you were alright." Ben paused and shifted his feet. "The only thing was, O'Grady was thrown from his horse and busted his leg."

Mrs. O'Grady looked as if she was about to faint. "How is he now?"

"Oh, he's okay now." Ben shoved his hands into his pockets. "We been camped about one mile away for about a day now, waiting for him to get well enough to stand without fainting."

"Thank you," Mrs. O'Grady murmured quietly.

"We saw your campfire," Ben continued, "and Joel sent me over to see who it was."

"And nearly got yourself killed," Elizabeth finished.

"Yep," Ben grinned. "I nearly did at that."

"Tomorrow we'll come over to your camp," Jolene said, resting the butt of the shotgun on the ground and nodding toward Mrs. O'Grady. "That's Mr. O'Grady's wife."

Ben tipped his hat at Mrs. O'Grady, but looked confused. "How.."

"Ask Mr. O'Grady," Jolene put in. "I'm sure he'll tell you his story and tomorrow Mrs. O'Grady will tell you hers. Right now, it'd probably be best if you returned your camp so we can get some sleep."

Ben nodded and turned to go, his eyes lingering on Elizabeth. "See you tomorrow." Then he was gone, crashing through the brush back toward his camp.

About at quiet as a grizzly bear, Jolene thought disgustedly.

"You weren't very nice," Elizabeth said reproachfully when he had gone.

Jolene looked at her with a hint of disbelief. "I was as nice as I could be when I wasn't even sure I could trust him. And besides, if I hadn't told him to leave, he'd've stayed all night."

"Well, it's dangerous out there," Elizabeth said, casting a furtive glance into the dark trees.

"He has a handgun tucked in his belt. And I don't have respect for a near grown man who's afraid of the dark."

Elizabeth was quiet as they crawled back into their beds. Jolene could hear Mrs. O'Grady soothing Sean back to sleep. Then she heard Elizabeth whisper her name. "Jolene?"

"What?" Jolene whispered back.

"What did you really think of Ben?"

Jolene thought for a minute. "I don't know yet," she said finally. "It's kind of hard to tell. He seemed nice."

"He is nice," Elizabeth murmured.

"Good night," Jolene said quickly, trying to steer her thoughts away.
"G'night."

But now, Jolene was certain: Elizabeth liked Ben.

Jolene was up at dawn, starting the fire again and hitching the horses to the wagon. It wasn't long before Mrs. O'Grady was awake and had breakfast cooking.

Elizabeth woke to the smell of coffee. Stretching, she pushed her brown hair out of her eyes. "I dreamed about Ben," she said quietly, almost to herself.

Jolene's black eyes met her sister's blue-gray ones, and a look of silent understanding passed between them..

It wasn't long before they were on the road again, following it toward a thin column of smoke rising above the trees about a mile away. Mrs. O'Grady was cheerful and talkative. Sean too, was talkative as they made there way through a stand of hickory.

At a curve in the road, there was a path that branched off, covered with hoof prints. They followed it until they reached a clearing, then Esperanza nickered. There came an answering whinny from the campfire in the small clearing. There were three horses tied to a tree at the edge. On a log, sat Ben and two other people; a woman and a man. On a bedroll beside them lay a still figure.

The three on the log looked up as the wagon rolled to a stop. Both Ben and the other young man, who Jolene assumed was Joel, started for the wagon as they pulled to a stop.

Joel was a bit taller and bigger built than Ben, but otherwise they could have been mistaken for twins. They were both handsome, Jolene thought, now that she saw them in the light. They had gray eyes and sandy hair that needed trimming. They were both dressed almost identically.

Ben reached the wagon first and reached up to help Elizabeth down. Joel helped Mrs. O'Grady down and Jolene quickly jumped down and turned to help Sean. The small boy clung to her hand as he looked at the strange faces and Jolene could feel him trembling.

They walked to the campfire and introductions were made. Eulalia was a petite young woman with large gray eyes and lighter colored sandy hair than her brothers.

Then, they turned to look at O'Grady. The only part of him that showed from underneath the blanket was his face. It was deathly pale. He didn't look as if he was breathing.

"We should probably let him sleep a bit," Joel said quietly, crouching down beside him and feeling for a pulse. "He scarcely slept last night when he heard his wife was coming. He didn't—"

Joel stopped talking and suddenly pulled back the blanket and laid his ear on O'Grady's chest. He stood up slowly, his face grim. "I can't feel a pulse. Or a heartbeat. I...I don't think he's alive any longer. I'm truly sorry, Mrs. O'Grady." His voice grew softer. "I'm truly sorry."

Then, everyone fell deathly silent, only to have the silence broken by Sean's sobs. "No, Da, no! Don't die again!"

CHAPTER NINE

Mrs. O'Grady knelt beside her little boy and let the tears stream down her cheeks. Jolene's own eyes blurred with tears and she sensed Elizabeth's shoulders start to shake with silent sobs.

Jolene put her arm around Elizabeth as hot tears spilled over her cheeks. All their hard searching for nothing. Now O'Grady was dead and would never see his wife or son.

Joel and Ben stood rather awkwardly, and Eulalia let tears stream freely down her cheeks.

Was life always so full of loss, Jolene wondered as the tears came faster. Did life always change so drastically?

"What's all the tears fer?" The voice came out in a hoarse whisper.

Everyone looked down at O'Grady, who was now sitting up on his blanket, his legs stretched out awkwardly in front of him. He blinked blue eyes. "Meagan, is that you?"

With a half-smothered sob, Meagan O'Grady turned and nearly leaped into Daniel O'Grady's arms. Sean, who had stopped crying, suddenly smiled and put small arms as far around his parents as they could go. Mr. O'Grady fell back onto the blanket, his wife and son in his arms.

The other five stared at the trio in amazement.

"Am I seeing things," Joel said incredulously, "or did he just regain life?"

"If you're seeing things, then so'm I," Ben replied, a huge grin splitting his face.

Suddenly, they started laughing and Elizabeth squeezed Jolene so hard it hurt. "I guess the O'Grady's will see each other after all!" she cried.

"I guess so!" Jolene cried back, giddy with happiness.

Mr. O'Grady finally managed to sit up, an arm around his wife, the other around his son. "Will somebody please tell me what all the commotion is about? A body can't sleep around here, what with all the noise!"

A few days later, the whole group was back in town. O'Grady planned on staying in town for a while before heading off again to find a job. He was even thinking of finding a job in town and buying a small house on the outskirts.

The Wheatstalks were going to head out for Kansas. The day they left town, Elizabeth broke down and cried. She had promised to write to Ben, and to try to give him an address. He'd given her a brotherly hug and then had left. The day they left was Elizabeth's thirteenth birthday.

Jolene knew she was taking it hard when the wagon rolled out of town, but she didn't know what to do.

Jolene and Elizabeth decided to stay in the hotel room beside the O'Gradys for a few days. But soon Jolene began to get restless. She didn't like the bustle of town life and was homesick for the grassy meadows and tall rocky mountains of their ranch.

One night as the girls were brushing their hair and getting ready for bed, Jolene announced an idea that had been stuck in her head the whole day. "I want to go home, Elizabeth. I just can't take this life anymore."

Elizabeth stopped mid-brush, her mouth dropping open. "Home? But it's burned to the ground!"

Jolene's heart ached at the memory of ashes and charred boards that was once her home. Would she be able to brave that scene again? She made up her mind. "I want to go back. We can stay in the barn and look for some jobs in town. As long as you're willing, I want to go back."

Elizabeth sat still for a minute, deep in thought. "I want to go back," she said finally. "I think we can do it."

"We'll leave tomorrow," Jolene said firmly, flipping her long braid over her shoulder.

"I wish I could be more like you, Jolene," Elizabeth said, suddenly wistful. "You're so brave and you always seem to know what you're doing."

Jolene sat, surprised for a moment, then she recovered. "That's only on the outside, Elizabeth. Inside I'm just as scared and unsure of things as you are."

The next day, after a quarrel with the O'Gradys, the girls saddled Esperanza, and with what little supplies they had, they mounted, ready to leave the little town behind. Mrs. O'Grady bid them goodbye with a catch in her voice. "We'll never forget you girls," she said tearfully.

"Remember," Mr. O'Grady put in. "We're always here if you need some friends."

Jolene nodded, forcing back tears. "We'll write if we can. We gave you the address. Let us know if you ever find the person who blackmailed you with those letters."

Elizabeth was crying when they left town, her cheek against Jolene's shoulder. "Why does life have to be so full of goodbyes?" she said, her voice breaking in the middle of the sentence. "It's enough to break a person's heart."

Jolene didn't have an answer.

It took them three days of searching and lost trails and aching muscles from riding all day, but they found their hometown. They passed the bank as they rode through, and Jolene remembered the man's excuse about not being able to pass money out to just anybody.

It was late afternoon when they reached the ranch. It still looked the same as when they had left it. It was heart-wrenching to see it again and remember that awful night, but no tears would come. There was only an aching hollowness.

The girls dismounted and Jolene led Esperanza to the barn and let her loose in a stall. Then, taking a deep breath, she looked at Elizabeth. "I want to walk around the house to see if I can find anything."

Elizabeth swallowed and nodded. She followed Jolene out of the barn into the sunlight. The mountains towering above the trees were as blue as ever, and the meadows were as green. For a minute, Jolene just drank it all in, glad to see something familiar, realizing what "Home" really meant.

Then the girls went forward toward the house. The porch had collapsed overtop of itself and the girls had to be careful not to step on shards of broken glass with their bare feet. Most of the chimney was still standing, a big stack of stones coming out of the rubble, like something that had just refused to go down. The girls skirted around to the side of the house where their parents' bedroom window had been. The shutters lay in one piece on the ground, latched.

Jolene frowned. Pa never latched the shutters from the outside. The people who had burnt the place down must have latched them to make sure no one could get out. She felt anger rush into her like a swift mountain stream. She would never be able to understand how a human being could do something so cruel.

Then came the back of the house. There was something on the ground beside the foundation. Elizabeth bent to pick it up. It was a shoe, one of Sammie's little boots. It was now blackened and charred, but the laces were like new. Elizabeth handled it gently, as if it were alive, something of Sammie's to remember him by.

The next thing they saw was a feather pillow. Jolene had no idea why it hadn't burned. Jolene remembered throwing a crow feather into the fire once. Feathers always burned fast, giving off an acrid smell. Jolene picked the pillow up and carried it with her. It was still white and smelled like lye soap.

That was all they found. The rest of the house was just ashes and charred pieces of things. The girls made their way to the barn in the dusky twilight, each silent, remembering things from their childhood. They were no longer children, Jolene reflected. Tragedy had forced them into adulthood and there was no turning back.

In the barn, Jolene and Elizabeth sat in a straw-filled stable, and though they weren't hungry, they ate some jerky. Jolene was about to get up and go outside to fill their canteen in the nearby stream that Jim and Pete used to fish in. Then they heard a noise. A loud thud in the hayloft. Then something clinked.

The girls stared at each other, reading fear in each other's eyes. What would happen to them next? Would they ever be able to go somewhere without being in danger?

CHAPTER TEN

Elizabeth opened her mouth to speak, then closed it. Jolene picked up the shotgun and sat with it on her lap, pointing it toward the stall door. There was silence. The two girls sat tense and waiting.

Then, there came rustling sounds from the loft and the creak of someone—or more than one person?—descending the ladder. Jolene's finger slid onto the trigger as a shadow appeared near the stall's open door. Then a figure in the dusty clothing of a rancher, and two guns tied at his thighs, appeared in the opening of the stall. His legs were bowed from years in the saddle and his face was weathered and wrinkled. White hair stuck out from under his hat.

Elizabeth recognized him first. "Uncle Craig!"

"Lizzie! Lena! You're alive!"

The two girls stood, Jolene letting the shotgun slide to the floor as he swept them into a bear hug. When he stepped back, his blue-gray eyes were misty. "Where's the rest of the family?"

The girls looked at each other, then back at Uncle Craig. "They burned with the house."

Uncle Craig lowered his wiry frame down in the straw. "Tell me the story. All of it. Now."

They did, in as little words as possible, and with dry eyes.

A few tears had fallen down Uncle Craig's face by the time they had finished. For a minute, they just sat in silence. Jolene studied her uncle. He was her father's older brother, older by several years. He and his wife Sophie hadn't been able to have any children, and had moved to Oregon five years ago.

What were they doing—he doing—in Colorado? And where was Aunt Sophie?

It wasn't long before Uncle Craig spoke. "Your aunt and I wanted to come for a visit—we hadn't been since the war ended. So, we sent you a letter. We didn't get an answer, so we assumed it was okay to come. We pulled up to a burnt house."

"How is Aunt Sophie?" Elizabeth asked.

"She's doin' middlin' well. I left her in town while I came to have a look." He rose. "She'll be wantin' to see you. My horse is over in the trees."

It had been hard, but Jolene knew it was for the best. Elizabeth had wanted it, though she'd wanted Jolene to come with her. There had been tears and arguments. Now, it was settled and Jolene would not back down. She could not leave her home; the only one she had ever known, though it was burned to the ground. It was impossible to leave the Rockies and mountain streams, the meadows bright with flowers. No, she would stay in her own territory.

Elizabeth would go to Oregon with Uncle Craig and Aunt Sophie. There were no two ways about it. She would be safe and have a good home. Still, Jolene felt a sadness. It would be lonely without her sister, her best friend. She almost wished Uncle Craig and Aunt Sophie hadn't come at all. Then Elizabeth would still be with her.

But, it was going to be better this way. It had to be. Jolene hoped.

CHAPTER ELEVEN

A letter for you, Jolene," Mr. Smith the storekeeper announced.
Jolene stopped sweeping the floor and glanced up. It had been nearly a month since Elizabeth had left for Oregon with Uncle Craig and Aunt Sophie. It had been hard for Jolene. Very hard and lonely. Jolene hoped the letter was from Elizabeth.

Jolene had been working at the Dry Goods Store in town, and sleeping in a hotel room, paying with wages from the store. The ranch had been taken by tax collectors. Jolene still hadn't written Elizabeth about it because she didn't have an address. The only person she'd written to was O'Grady.

Now the storekeeper was holding out two letters. Jolene took them eagerly, scanning the addresses. One from the O'Gradys and one from Elizabeth.

It only took Jolene a few minutes to finish sweeping, then she began straightening rows of candy jars on the counter. She could hardly wait for bedtime when she would be able to read the letters.

Dear Jolene, the one-page letter from O'Grady read.

We hope you are doing well, as we are all doing exceptionally well. My leg is almost completely healed and I am able to hobble around on crutches. Meagan and Sean are both looking healthier than when you last saw them— Sean has grown over an inch!

I can't express my happiness in finding my wife and son. I will forever be in debt to you for helping me find them.

I was sad to hear in your letter that you lost the ranch. I was also sad to hear that Elizabeth has gone to Oregon with your aunt and uncle. But, you can be sure you did the right thing. You are keeping her safe.

You must be brave throughout the months ahead, Jolene.

Meagan and Sean send much love. We hope to see you again sometime. Don't be afraid to come to us if you need something.

Your friend,
Daniel O'Grady.

Jolene lay the letter aside, glad to hear of good health and good spirits. Then, eagerly, she opened Elizabeth's letter.

Dear Jolene,

I miss you. Very much. Right now, as I'm writing this, Fort Bridger is a speck on the horizon among the trees. I'm tired of riding on the wagon seat or walking beside the wagon. I wish I was home.

Aunt Sophie and Uncle Craig are really nice. I made a friend too. Her name is Clara Osborne and she's thirteen. She has blonde hair and blue eyes and she's very shy—not to me, but to boys and grownups. Just the other night, Chase Walters asked her to take a walk with him, and she just turned bright red and shook her head. He asked me, then, and I said no. But I think I said it a little too mean because Aunt Sophie frowned at me. But I couldn't help it. He teases all the girls and makes a general pest of himself. And he's ugly.

I wish you were here. Remember how much fun we used to have at school, making fun of the boys when we were supposed to be doing math? We sat together in one desk, and you always drew the best pictures on the slate. I couldn't help giggling sometimes. Remember the time the teacher started over toward us and you turned the boy's head into a zero, his body into a plus sign and his legs into an eleven? That was one I drew and the teacher never suspected.

Oh, I almost forgot! Happy Birthday early (or late). I wish I could be there—or you here. You won't have anyone to spend your birthday with.

Did you hear from O'Grady? I hope they're doing alright.

Aunt Sophie and Uncle Craig send you their love. I think Aunt Sophie's a little frustrated because you wouldn't come with us. Uncle Craig understands. He says he had a feeling you wouldn't want to leave your home.

As soon as I'm done with this letter, I'm going to write to Ben. He can't write to me now because he doesn't know that I'm on the Oregon Trail. It's sad to think I'll only be able to write letters for a while, and not read them.

Jolene, how old was Mama when she met pa? I was thinking about that last night and Uncle Craig wasn't sure. Do you ever want to marry? I do. I would like to marry someone like Ben. I suppose it's silly of me to be thinking of marriage, me being only thirteen, but I was just thinking.

I hope you're doing well and have a good job. I miss you. Write me a letter and send it to Aunt Sophie's address in Oregon. Maybe it will be there when I reach Oregon. It seems strange to be traveling like this. I wonder what Oregon looks like?

Love,
Elizabeth

Jolene leaned back on the bed and looked out her hotel room window at the starry night sky. It seemed strange to hear wagons going by in the middle of the night, and saloon music and laughter. Sometimes it was hard to sleep.

Jolene put the letters on the small stand beside her bed, and put out the lamp, pulling the covers up to her chin. She was glad everyone was okay. The letters had made her miss them even more.

She was just drifting off to sleep when she heard footsteps outside the door. The handle rattled. She'd forgotten to lock it!

The door opened easily as a tall shadowy figure stepped into the room. Jolene lay still, watching through her lashes as the person closed the door and glanced around the room. Light from the street fell on his snakeskin boots and silver spurs.

The figure glanced around the room, and Jolene hardly dared breathe. Then, the man made his way over to the small closet at the end of the room, and slipped inside, his spurs jingling.

Jolene wished she had the shotgun, but it was under the bed. She couldn't get it without disturbing the man. Why had he come in anyway? Was he running from someone? He hadn't seemed in a hurry.

Jolene listened, but could hear no other footsteps outside. The room was silent. She could hear his breathing.

Stealthily, Jolene moved her one hand out of the blankets, down toward the floor. If she could only reach the shotgun…

The man shifted his feet, spurs clinking again. Jolene heard the sound of a gun being drawn from leather. She forced her body to relax and she squeezed her eyes shut.

Don't think about anything but sleep, she told herself. *With sleep, you aren't aware of anything that's going on around you.*

Jolene sent up a quick prayer, then tried to think of absolutely nothing but sleep.

The next thing she knew, Jolene opened her eyes to morning sunlight. Cautiously, she rolled over. The closet door stood wide open. She looked over at the bedroom door. It, too, was wide open. Getting out of bed, Jolene shut the bedroom door and locked it. As she turned back to her bed, She suddenly realized—her letters from O'Grady and Elizabeth were gone! The man had taken them!

CHAPTER TWELVE

Jolene felt anger boiling up inside her. Why would anybody want to steal her letters? She dressed quickly, then left the room, locking it behind her. The man could still be in town—even in the hotel. And, Jolene wanted those letters back.

Her bare feet barely made a sound on the steps as she made her way down the stairs. Only a few people were in the lobby, and none of them wore snakeskin boots with spurs.

Jolene slipped out of the hotel and crossed the street to the general store. Maybe Mr. Smith had seen the man.

The bell over the door jingled as Jolene entered the store. Mr. Smith had a customer, so Jolene stepped aside to wait.

The May air was warm and Jolene was glad for her cotton dress and braided hair. It was surely going to be warm. Her eyes scanned the room absently as she waited. Her glance stopped at the man.

He was short, yet stocky, dressed in dusty clothes and Jolene couldn't see his face. He shifted then, and a jingle made Jolene glance. Snakeskin boots! Jolene's heart lurched. So this was the man who had stolen her letters! Before she could think of what to do next, the bell tinkled behind her, and someone else entered the store.

Jolene backed a little farther back into the shadows and pretended to be straightening some jars of pickles. Spurs jingled as the newcomer strode up to the counter, stopping beside the stocky man. They wore identical boots!

Which one was it, Jolene wondered. Tall and skinny, or short and stocky?

She was lost in her thoughts until the tall one's voice penetrated her pondering. "Kin ya tell us how long it takes ta git ta the town of Salida? Thet's were we're headed an' we ain't nivver bin up there afore."

Mr. Smith seemed to think for a minute. "Coupla days mebbe. Have kin up there?"

"Uh…" the tall man began. The stocky one elbowed him.

"Nope. We jes got some business to take care of, that's all."

Mr. Smith nodded. "I see. Well, you fellers have nice day. I need to git back to work."

Salida! That was where O'Grady was staying!

The men turned from the counter and had started for the door with their bundles in their arms, when they caught sight of Jolene.

For a second, the tall man's black eyes locked with Jolene's and she glared at him. Something changed in the man's eyes and for a second his face turned ugly.

Then, both men smiled coolly, tipped their hats, and were gone.

Salida! The word pounded in Jolene's head. They must have taken the letters from her, seen O'Grady's address, and decided to—to what? Jolene had no idea. What would they want with O'Grady?

Jolene sighed and turned back to straightening the jars on the shelves. But, her conscience wouldn't let her think of anything but those men. Were they going to hurt O'Grady? Were they his friends?

Jolene pushed away the thoughts and went to find the storekeeper so he could tell her what to do next.

By the time Jolene went to the hotel that night, she'd made up her mind. She had to find out whether those men were O'Grady's friends or foes.

The next morning Jolene packed her few belongings in the old pillowcase. She carefully counted her wages from the night before when she had told Mr. Smith that she would be quitting. Then she tucked the money into the pouch at her waist, where she kept Elizabeth's derringer. The money wasn't much, but it would have to do. She had to quit her job.

Jolene wished she could just send a letter, but she knew it wouldn't get there in time. She would ride Esperanza.

She went out of town in the direction of Salida, keeping Esperanza at a fast clip.

There weren't any noticeable fresh prints, for it had rained the night before. And besides that, riders had left town after the two snakeskin booted men had, and covered the tracks.

Jolene enjoyed the feeling of sitting on a horse's back, realizing she'd missed riding Esperanza. The horse, too, was eager to go, after a few days with nothing but a corral for exercise. For a while Jolene let her run, then slowed her again to a clip. She didn't want to tire her too soon.

They traveled all day without stopping and when they did stop, it was at the remains of a campfire. Both girl and horse were dead tired.

Jolene spread her blanket under a tree, not bothering to build a fire or to eat anything. She tied Esperanza's reins around her wrist and laid down. Within seconds, Jolene was asleep, the shotgun beside her.

The next day was warm and muggy. Jolene didn't push Esperanza, but let her take her own pace.

The clouds were gray and the sky looked like rain. Jolene would have welcomed rain. She was sweating in the sticky air. Then a cool breeze blew, and she could smell a storm. There was a low rumble in the distance. Esperanza laid her ears back.

Jolene groaned aloud. Esperanza could handle gun shots and barking dogs, even the howl of wolves and coyotes, but she spooked during thunderstorms. Jolene pulled Esperanza to a stop and slid off her back. She realized as she led the horse to a tree, that this was the same spot that Elizabeth had been "kidnapped."

Tying the reins to a branch, she tried to soothe Esperanza. The whites of the horse's eyes showed and her ears were laid back. The breeze blew Jolene's hair and skirts and ruffled Esperanza's mane. Thunder rumbled again, this time louder. Rain began to fall, softly at first, then harder. Before long, it was so hard it stung. Esperanza reared as thunder cracked and boomed. Rain pelted them as Jolene struggled to keep the horse under control.

Then, the rain turned to hail stones, large and white, stinging even more than the rain had. Jolene had the reins untied from the tree and now had a hold of Esperanza's head, hanging onto her to keep her from rearing. The horse's shrill whinny hurt Jolene's ears.

And then, the storm stopped. The hail no longer stung them, but lay an inch thick on the ground. The clouds rolled away to reveal a clear blue sky.

Esperanza calmed. Jolene relaxed. Now that the storm was over, her wet clothes felt good in the hot air. Mounting, she kicked Esperanza into a trot and they started off again. There was a knot in the pit of Jolene's stomach as they turned onto the well-used road. They had taken a short cut through the woods.

Now, for all Jolene knew, they could be ahead of the two men in the snakeskin boots. Jolene didn't cotton to the idea of having the men behind her, at her back. She wouldn't be able to see them if they were to sneak up behind her.

It was the next morning that Jolene began recognizing land marks that told her they were close to town. They had just rounded a curve when Jolene sensed something. She pulled Esperanza to a stop in the middle of the road. The horse rolled her eyes and danced in place. It was too late for Jolene to realize she had made a mistake in pulling Esperanza to a stop.

Then, there was the sharp crack of a rifle, and Jolene felt pain. She fell from the Esperanza as the horse crumpled to her knees and gave a shrill scream of pain.

Jolene lay motionless in the dirt road as the horse's legs churned up dust.

CHAPTER THIRTEEN

The way Pa had taught her, Jolene tucked and rolled as Esperanza went down. There was an excruciating pain in her right leg and Jolene lay still as the shot echoed through the forest. Then Esperanza's shrill cries of pain filled the air.

Jolene heard footsteps, but didn't dare move as she lay on her side in the dirt, eyes closed. She felt warm sticky blood running down her leg from the bullet wound.

The footsteps stopped behind her and she felt a boot toe nudge her back. Spurs jingled. In one movement, Jolene rolled, raised the derringer, and squeezed the trigger. The gun went off and the tall man in snakeskin boots stumbled back, yelling as blood spurted from his shoulder.

Jolene was on her feet, trembling. She had never shot anyone before. And quickly, she decided she didn't want to do it again.

The man was glaring at her now and Jolene couldn't keep her mind on what he was saying. Her leg was throbbing and her foot was covered with blood. Esperanza's whinnies seemed far away. Blackness started to creep up in the corners of Jolene's vision and she felt dizzy

Then, blackness covered everything and she fell.

When Jolene opened her eyes, all she could see was blackness. For a second, she panicked. Had she gone blind? She strained her eyes to see into the darkness. It took a few minutes before she could make out some shadowy forms looming above her. Where was she?

She sat up, and her head throbbed. The ground was solid rock. Were they rocks looming above her? Jolene stood and leaned against one, her leg now almost numb with pain. They were rocks alright. And they weren't about to budge. Jolene limped along the rocks, trying to find an opening. There was none.

By now Jolene realized she was in a cave of some sort and there was no way out. "I need help," she said aloud, her voice echoing in the shadowy darkness. "Help," she said it louder. There was nothing but echoes.

Fear clutched her as she listened. The echoes sent chills up and down her arms. Covering her ears with her hands, Jolene screamed, "*Help!*"

As she took her hands away, a funny feeling came into the pit of her stomach. Dirt began sifting down from the roof of the cave. Then something creaked and there was a low rumble. Jolene froze, expecting the whole cave to crumble in around her.

But then there was silence. Jolene was afraid to move for fear of a cave-in. She wasn't so sure it was a cave after all. It could be an old mine shaft. And that could be even more dangerous.

Jolene wished with all her heart that she hadn't left town. She wished even more that she'd never even seen the men with the snakeskin boots.

Jolene sat down on the floor and cautiously leaned against a rock wall, pulling her one knee up and arranging her skirts. She wondered if the O'Gradys were alright. She hoped so. It would be her fault if the men in the snakeskin boots hurt them.

But why would they want the letters? Then, it hit her. They must have been the men who blackmailed O'Grady and his wife! It had to be! Now they had somehow found out the O'Gradys were back together and that Jolene was a friend.

A sudden pain shot through Jolene's leg and she bit her lip to keep from crying out. She had to get out of the cave, but there was absolutely no way with her leg the way it was. The rock walls were straight and smooth, up and down, with no toe holds, and they reached above her head.

Jolene felt like giving up. How could she ever live another day in this cave with no food, water, or help?

It had taken Harp Reddick five days to finally get from Utah, across the border, to the upper mid-corner of Colorado territory. Now he rode toward the magnificent Rockies that rose above him. They were very different from the canyonlands that he was used to.

But now that he saw the Rockies, he wished he'd spent his life in Colorado instead of southwestern Utah. There was something about the place…

His blue eyes scanned the line of trees that began a dense forest of pine. In all his twenty years, he'd never seen anything so breathtaking as the scene before him. Now, his family was dead. There was no one to hold him back from anything.

All he owned in the world was with him, his horse and saddle, the dusty ranching clothes on his back, his guns tied at his thighs, the bit of supplies in his saddlebags, and his bedroll. As far as he was concerned, it was all he needed. Then, Harp caught sight of two riders in the distance. The first humans he'd seen in two days. If they kept riding in that direction, his path and theirs were going to intersect.

Wincing as he shifted his shoulder, Hank Williams glanced over at Willie Monroe. There was a rider coming toward them.

Willie's face was expressionless, but his eyes were on the lone rider. Why would someone be out riding alone? He felt uneasy. It could be the law.

His spurs jingled as he kicked his horse faster. Hank did the same.

As the lone rider drew closer, Hank could see his tied down guns. The rider was tall and broad shouldered and sat easy in the saddle. He rode a tall gray horse and his hat was pulled low.

Hank sensed him watching them.

Jolene jumped when she heard the gunshot. At first she thought she could have imagined it. Maybe it was just wishful thinking.

Minutes slowly dragged by. Then Jolene heard something inside the cave, rattling loose rocks. Footsteps.

Jolene stood. She couldn't be any worse off if she yelled.

"Help!" the echoes bounced off the walls.

"Where are you?" It was a man's voice—could it be that the men with the snakeskin boots had come back?

"Here! Behind the rocks! I can't get out!"

The footsteps turned and went out again, and Jolene's spirits sank. Was he leaving? Then she heard the sound of a horse being led in, and the creak of leather as someone mounted.

"Easy, easy." The voice was calming.

The next thing Jolene knew, there was man crouched on top of one of the rocks, just a dim outline against the darkness.

"If I give you my hand, can you reach it?" he questioned.

"I—I think so." Reaching up, Jolene felt a large strong hand grab hers. Then, another hand came down, and Jolene gripped it tightly. She wondered how he would ever be able to pull her up—she wasn't exactly light. But then she felt her feet lift up off the ground.

There was a sharp pain in her leg, and for a second, she thought she was going to black out.

"Don't let go!" the man's voice came dimly, and then she was sitting on the wide rock beside him, her leg throbbing.

Glancing to her left, the sunshine made her eyes water from the brightness.

"Okay?" the man asked.

Jolene nodded. Sure she was okay. As long as she could leave the cave, she would be okay.

The man was sliding down the rock now, and Jolene realized he was very tall. His head reached the top of the rock, while hers had been a foot short. He reached up to help her, and Jolene slid down. When he released his hands from her waist, Jolene put pressure on her leg. It was all she could do to keep from screaming. Then, all went black.

When Jolene opened her eyes, she was laying on a bedroll, with her leg in a bandage of what looked like ripped shirts.

There was a man with his hat pulled low, poking the smoldering fire with a stick.

Where was she, and what had happened? All around her was woods, and it was late afternoon. A tall gray horse was tied to a tree behind the man. Both man and horse were covered with dust.

The man tossed the stick away and rubbed his chin as if in thought. Then he looked over at her. Even from where she lay, Jolene could see that his eyes were very blue.

"Howdy," he said, seemingly making no effort to sound friendly.

"Where am I and why?" Jolene's voice came out barely more than a whisper.

"You're in Colorado as far as I can see it, and I sure don' know why."

Jolene felt her temper start to rise. What kind of answer was that? She thought hard for a minute before she could remember what had happened to her. Then it came back. Those men, the cave…this must be the man who had helped her out. "Who are you?" she asked aloud.

"Harp Reddick." The man took his hat off, and Jolene realized he was younger than she'd thought. Twenty maybe. He was looking at her as if expecting her to say her name.

"I'm Jolene Culhaine. Why did you help me?" It slipped out before she could stop it.

Harp put his hat back on. "What was I supposed to do, leave you?"

"How did you know I was in there?"

"Tracks. An' your horse out front."

Esperanza! "Where is my horse?" Jolene asked, dreading the answer.

"Dead."

"Did you shoot her?"

Harp tugged his hat lower and stood, looking off into the woods. "Yep. Had to."

Jolene thought for a minute before sitting up. "Did you see two men on your way here?"

"Yep. Wearin' fancy boots an' spurs."

Jolene stood, her hair cascading down her back. Her leg hurt, but not enough to stop her.

The man glanced at her. "Are you injun?"

Jolene lifted her chin. "Yes."

"Thought so. I lived with the injuns for a time when I was young."

At least he didn't have anything against Indians. He wasn't friendly though. He wasn't hostile enough to make her afraid, but he most surely didn't make her comfortable. Should she ask him? "Could you..." she hesitated. "Would you be able to take me to town?"

"Don't know what else to do with you," he retorted. "Where's the nearest town?"

Jolene stiffened. "You can just leave me here if you want. If I'm really that much trouble. I didn't *want* all this to happen!"

The man took a step forward, looming above her. Despite herself, Jolene gulped at the sight of the guns tied down at his thighs.

Then, to her surprise, he smiled. "Guess I deserved that."

"Yes, you did." Jolene's words slipped out again.

This time, he laughed. "I'll take you to town," he said. "Guess you really couldn't help it, being trapped in a cave."

Then his expression changed. "How'd you get in there an' who shot your leg?"

"The men with the fancy boots."

Harp's eyes narrowed and Jolene noticed a scar on his jaw. "Why?" The word came out short and clipped.

"I was following them."

"Why?"

"They're going to kill the O'Gradys and I need to get to town before they do." Even as she said it, Jolene realized she was probably too late to even warn O'Grady. If only she had been more careful, she wouldn't have gotten shot...

"Which way to town?" Harp's words broke into her thoughts.

"East."

"Let's go."

Despite the pain in her leg, Jolene managed to swing up behind Harp.

They didn't talk until the town was in sight. By then it was dark, with only stars and a moon to light their way.

"Won't your family be worried about you?" Harp asked.

"My family's dead."

They were silent. Jolene knew the men in the snakeskin boots were already in town. How would she warn O'Grady? She couldn't ask Harp to stay in town because he was going...where was he going?

"Where were you headed when you found me?" Jolene asked.

"I was goin' nowhere."

As they neared town, Jolene heard the tinkling sound of a piano, and the sound of voices and laughter.

Where would the O'Gradys be? Would they even be alive? Jolene could only pray.

CHAPTER FOURTEEN

Harp pulled up to a hitching rail in front of Dingham's Hotel. Light spilled out of the windows, making bright squares on the ground outside.

Harp rested the palms of his hands on his gun butts. "Okay, now," he said in a low voice, his eyes scanning the boardwalk for signs of the two men in snakeskin boots. "I want you to go to the Dry Goods store over there and inquire on the whereabouts of your friends—just be careful no one overhears—and make sure those men don't see you. The name's O'Grady, right?"

Jolene nodded.

"Okay," he said, looking down at her, his face shadowed. "I'm going to take a look in the saloons for those two men."

Was he going to get drunk, and then leave her? Jolene watched him stride off. She hoped not. Jolene headed for the Dry Goods store, moving quickly through the shadows. It wasn't late yet, so people were still strolling the boardwalks.

There was no one in the Dry Goods store but the owner, who was dusting off the candy shelves. He turned as she entered. "Hello, miss. Can I help you?"

Jolene managed a smile. "Hello. I was wondering if you could tell me of the whereabouts of the O'Gradys."

"There certainly are a lot of people coming in today who want to know the whereabouts of the O'Gradys. The O'Gradys live down the road past the school house. Little white house. Couldn't miss it."

"Thank you." Jolene turned to go.

"Miss?"

Jolene turned back. "Yes?"

"If you're going to wait until morning, Danny'll be in town. He's part of a carpentry business down the street."

"Thank you." Jolene left and started back to Harp's horse. He hadn't told her where to meet him when she was done.

Jolene reached the horse and stood impatiently waiting for Harp to come back. It was a bit scary waiting in the dark, knowing that two killers were out there.

Jolene thought about what the storekeeper had said, *There certainly are a lot of people coming in today who want to know the whereabouts of the O'Gradys.* Did that mean that the two men in the snakeskin boots had asked the storekeeper too?

A shadow fell across her from behind, and Jolene whirled, expecting to see a man in snakeskin boots standing in front of her. But it was only Harp.

"Well?" he asked.

"They live just out of town, past the schoolhouse."

He nodded. "We'll stay in the hotel for the night."

"Did you find anything out?" Jolene was anxious.

He lowered his voice. "They're going to ambush O'Grady tomorrow morning as soon as he leaves for work, then they're gonna leave the kid tied in a sack under a bed, and take the missus with them."

"How did you find out?"

They were heading into the hotel now.

"Overheard 'em in a saloon."

Jolene hoped it was true. Right now, she was depending on Harp's word to save the O'Grady's lives.

After an argument about who was going to pay, Harp got two rooms and they went upstairs.

Harp unlocked Jolene's room first, then lit a lamp and pulled the curtains closed. He caught Jolene eyeing him uneasily as he moved around the room, looking in the closet and under the bed.

"Never can be too safe," he said. He could see the girl still didn't trust him. He handed her the key. "Keep the door locked. If someone breaks in, yell."

"How will they know we're here?"

"Might recognize my horse, or someone might tell them. As of now, they think I'm riding east and you're dead in the cave." He turned to leave.

"Mr. Reddick—"

He turned. "Harp."

"Harp," Jolene repeated. "What are we going to do to help the O'Gradys?"

"I got a plan."

"What?"

He grinned. "I'm not sure yet." Then he was gone, shutting the door behind him.

Jolene sighed and slipped the key in the lock. It was hard to lock it, but Jolene finally got the key turned.

Then, she put out the lamp and slid into bed, pulling the covers up to her chin.

Sleep would not come. The room was dark and Jolene's eyes were not yet accustomed to it.

Just as Jolene was beginning to feel drowsy, she heard footsteps coming down the hall toward her room. There was the familiar dreaded sound of spurs jingling. Suddenly Jolene was wide awake.

The footsteps stopped outside her door. More footsteps were coming. Spurs jingled. The door handle rattled. Jolene tensed. Honestly, she would never sleep in a hotel room again. There was the sound of metal scraping metal, and the key fell out of its hole and onto the floor in Jolene's room. Jolene wished for the derringer that had somehow gotten lost that day in the cave.

The door opened. Two figures were silhouetted against the doorway. Jolene recalled Harp's words, "If someone breaks in, yell."

But she didn't want to wake everyone in the hotel, especially if the men weren't going to harm her.

The men slipped in, one of them almost knocking over the wash basin by the door. "Hank!" the other hissed, as he caught the pitcher, water sloshing onto the floor. "You clumsy ox! You're going to get us put in jail if you're not careful!"

The one named Hank closed the door carefully and put the key in his pocket without locking the door. "Sorry, Willie."

"You'd better be. Now, shut up and let's get the girl an' get oughtta here!"

They both started for the bed, one of them circling, spurs jingling, to the opposite side of the bed.

Jolene watched through half closed eyes, pretending to be asleep, but ready to fight the second one of them reached for her.

Suddenly, one halted. "Hank, did you lock the door?" he whispered.

"No," came the loud whisper back.

Jolene began to suspect Hank of being incredibly stupid.

"Well, lock it! All we need is for that gun-slingin' Reddick to come in here!"

Obediently, Hank tiptoed over to the door and reached into his shirt pocket for his key.

As he did so, the door handle turned and slowly swung open. Hank stared. Willie froze. Jolene was no longer pretending to be asleep, but had her eyes wide open. All three stared at the empty doorway.

"Close the door!" Willie hissed.

Hank reached out to close the door. As he did so, a tall figure appeared and stepped into the room, slamming a fist into Hank's face. Hank stumbled backwards, just missing the washstand.

Willie moved forward like a cat. The figure had closed the door and Willie moved in on him, drawing a large bladed knife from its sheath.

Jolene could barely see them. Slipping out of bed, she pulled back the curtains. Moonlight flooded the room, and Jolene saw Willie thrust the knife at Harp.

Jolene's breath caught in her throat. Harp's hand came up and grabbed Willie's wrist, twisting it behind his back. Jolene hear a cracking sound and Willie gave a yelp. Even in the moonlight, Jolene saw his face pale. Harp released his wrist and the knife clattered to the floor.

Harp smashed his left fist into Willie's face. Then his right fist. Then his left. Willie managed a solid punch on Harp's jaw before slumping to the floor, out cold.

Now Hank had risen, and lunged at Harp, the knife now in his hand. Harp ducked, ramming Hank in the stomach. The knife sliced Harp's shoulder and clattered to the floor again.

The two men both went for it. Harp reached it first, rolled over, and came up with the knife against Hank's throat. Hank backed up to the wall. Harp followed.

"Enough!" Hank gasped, his voice squeaking.

"Jolene, take his gun," Harp's voice was low with anger.

Jolene quickly took the gun and tossed it on the bed, doing the same with Willie's.

Harp lowered the knife and tucked it in his belt, breathing hard. His eyes were fastened on Hank. "What were you doing in this room?"

"Nothin'." Now that the knife wasn't against his throat, Hank was determined not to give anything away. "It's none o' your business."

"I'll make it my business!" Harp jammed one of his guns into Hank's stomach. "I want the truth, the whole truth, and I want it *now*!"

Jolene could read the fury in Harp's eyes.

Hank gulped.

"What were you doing in this room?" Harp's voice was steely. "You'd better talk if you don't want—"

"I'll talk!" Hank yelped.

"Talk!"

"Well," Hank rubbed his neck where the knife had rested. "We found out you two were in town, an' figgered you'd screw up our plans."

"The plans to rid the town of O'Gradys."

Hank broke out in a cold sweat. How had he known? "Yeah. So we came fer the girl an' sent the rest of the gang to the O'Gradys."

The rest of the gang! Jolene's heart hit the floor. The O'Grady's were as good as dead, and there was not a thing she could do about it.

CHAPTER FIFTEEN

"Jolene, grab a gun an' keep it trained on Hank," Harp spoke quickly.

Jolene took both guns from the bed and trained them on Hank. She wished Harp would tell her his plans. She watched as he holstered his gun and reached down to pick Willie up by his belt. Jolene was amazed at his strength. Willie was not a small man.

"Let's go." Harp led the way out of the room and down the stairs to the front desk.

The owner rushed out of his bedroom, still in his long johns. "What's going on?"

"These two men caused a bit of trouble," Harp said calmly, "We're just takin' them to the sheriff's office. Then we'll be leavin' town."

The confused owner watched as Harp unlatched the front door and went out. Jolene and Hank followed, Jolene closing the door behind them.

Harp strode along the boardwalk, still holding Willie by his belt. A few late nighters stared as the small group passed.

It only took a few seconds to reach the sheriff's office.

Yawning, the sheriff moved from behind his desk to open a cell, his keys rattling as he searched for the right one.

Harp dumped Willie unceremoniously onto the hard floor. Hank gave them one final glare as he walked in. Harp stepped back as the sheriff shut the door. "You might want to go through their clothes."

The sheriff nodded. "Will do."

Harp headed for the door. Jolene almost had to run to catch up, tucking the two guns into the waistband of her skirts.

They reached Harp's horse, and he quickly untied it and mounted. Then, taking a foot out of the stirrup, he offered a hand to Jolene. Jolene heard him suck air between his teeth as she swung up.

"Harp, you're bleeding!" Jolene exclaimed.

"Yep," he gave her a grin, but it was forced. Jolene's heart flipped as his blue eyes met hers.

"Don't worry," he said at the expression on her face. "I'll be okay."

Jolene hoped so.

They rode out of town at a fast clip, with only the moon to guide them.

It wasn't long before they passed the little schoolhouse. Just around a curve in the road, they saw the light of the O'Grady's house. Harp pulled the horse off the road and into the brush. "We'll go on foot."

They dismounted and Harp tied the horse to a tree. They made their way through the shadowy woods to the house.

There were three masked men in the yard, all on horseback. O'Grady stood with his hands tied behind his back, and a noose around his neck. All four were gathered around a large cottonwood. Mrs. O'Grady and Sean weren't in sight.

At the edge of the woods, Harp turned to Jolene. "I want you to go around and see if you can get in the house without being seen. I'm going to start shooting. If anyone's inside besides the woman and the boy, keep the gun trained on them. If they pull a gun, shoot 'em."

Jolene felt fear work it's way into the pit of her stomach, but she nodded. Turning, she started to make her way along the edge of the woods. She'd only gone a few steps when she heard Harp. "Jolene."

She turned. "What?"

"Be careful."

She couldn't see his face in the dark shadows. "I will."

Then, she began working her way around the house. She was nearly halfway when she heard, "Let 'im hang!"

She froze and glanced back at the figures illuminated by the light from an upstairs window. Then she heard a shot, and one rider fell from his horse.

Someone burst from the house's back door, a bundle in their arms, and made a dash for the woods.

Jolene hesitated. It was a man, that was for sure. He had pants on, so it couldn't be a woman. Jolene heard hoof beats and saw him riding away into the woods.

There were more shots as Jolene crept toward the house, praying for safety. When she reached the back door, she cautiously peered inside.

There was Mrs. O'Grady, gagged and tied to a chair. Her eyes widened as she caught sight of Jolene.

Cautiously, Jolene entered. Then, satisfied that no one else was there, she hurried over to Mrs. O'Grady and untied the gag and ropes.

Mrs. O'Grady just sat for a minute, rubbing her wrists as the gunshots outside continued. Then, suddenly, there was dead silence.

A few moments later, Jolene heard her name.

"Jolene!"

Was it Harp?

"Jolene, you can come out!"

Mrs. O'Grady and Jolene stepped outside into the cool night air. There were only two horses standing by the tree. The other could be seen galloping off into the darkness, riderless. The riders all lay on the ground.

Two men, O'Grady and Harp, stood under the tree. Jolene could tell Harp by his broad shoulders and height. He stood nearly a head taller than O'Grady.

O'Grady rubbed his neck where the noose had been. As the women came forward, Jolene could hear introductions being made.

Mrs. O'Grady went into her husband's arms. They held each other for a long moment. Jolene glanced at Harp. He had turned slightly away and was examining the cut on his shoulder.

"Is it bad?" Jolene asked softly. For the first time she caught full sight of the blood soaked shirt front.

He looked up, as if surprised to see her standing there. Harp shook his head. "Naaa." His eyes met hers. "You were pretty brave you know. Surprised at ya. Expected you to fall apart."

Jolene shook her head. "I was scared silly on the inside. I couldn't have done it without you."

He shrugged, then winced.

Mr. O'Grady had pulled back from his wife's embrace. "None of us could have done it without ye, Reddick. We're much obliged fer yer savin' our lives."

Harp tugged his hat brim lower and looked down at the bodies on the ground, as if he hadn't heard. "We'd best get these bodies to the sheriff—he'll want to look at them before the undertaker does."

O'Grady nodded toward a shed and small corral that Jolene hadn't noticed, on the other side of the house. "We got a wagon an' two horses in there."

"Bring it out."

Just as O'Grady was about to leave, Harp took off his hat and ran his fingers through his hair. "Hey, wasn't there a kid too?"

There was dead silence as the O'Gradys looked at each other. "Sean!"

Harp put his hat back on. "Check the house." All four started forward.

"We'll split up," Mrs. O'Grady said. "Jolene and…" she hesitated.

"Harp Reddick, ma'am."

"Yes, Harp, can look upstairs. Danny an' me'll check down here."

Harp and Jolene went up the stairs, and as they reached the top, Jolene remembered something. "Harp, when I was out there, someone came out the back door and rode away. He was carrying something."

Harp halted before a bedroom door. "Big enough to be the boy?"

"Yes."

"Well, let's look in the rooms up here. But I have a feelin' he ain't here."

"So do I."

It didn't take long to search all upstairs. Harp met Jolene at the top of the stairs, his face grim. Jolene didn't say a word, but just went down the stairs. Harp followed.

They met two equally somber faces at the bottom of the stairs.

"He ain't here." Harp spoke first.

"Where could he be?" O'Grady asked, his blue eyes worried.

"Jolene saw someone go out the back door when we arrived," Harp said. He didn't have to finish.

"Why were those men after you anyway?" Jolene asked, suddenly aware of the fact that she had no idea.

"Gold." O'Grady's voice was quiet. "I struck it rich a few years back an' when me wife an' me got separated, we both had gold. That's the reason fer blackmailing. Thought it'd be easier to get gold that way." His face darkened with anger. "Guess it didn't work."

Harp nodded. "Guess I'll be goin'." He turned for the door.

"Where?" Jolene was surprised. She hadn't thought he'd leave now…

"After the outlaw who took the kid." He disappeared out the door.

It took a second for it to sink in. Then, Jolene went after him.

He'd started across the yard toward the woods where his horse was tethered, when Jolene caught up with him. "Let me go with you."

He stopped. "No."

"Please?"

"No!"

"Why?" her eyes were pleading.

He looked away. "It's easier with one horse an' one rider. Kin travel faster."

"What if you get hurt?"

"I won't." he looked down at her, wondering what she would say next.

Jolene bit her lower lip, trying to think of another reason to make him change his mind. The next thing she knew, he'd pulled her to him. She could feel his strong heart beat through his shirt. He held her for a second, then released her. "I'll be back in a few days." Then he had all but disappeared into the darkness.

Jolene stood for a second, looking into the darkness, trying to catch a glimpse of him. But he was gone.

Her heart pounding, Jolene turned to go back to the house. Now she thought she knew how Elizabeth felt with Ben.

CHAPTER SIXTEEN

Jolene met worried faces as she stepped inside the O'Grady's house.
"He left?" Mr. O'Grady asked, searching her face.
Jolene nodded. "He's going to bring Sean back."

"You believe he kin." It was a statement, not a question.

Jolene bit her lower lip. "Yes, I guess I do."

"How did ye an' Harp get here?" Mrs. O'Grady asked curiously. "How did ye know we were in trouble?"

"Sit down an' tell us," Mr. O'Grady said, pulling out a kitchen chair.

Jolene sat down, realizing her legs had been trembling. She told the story to the O'Grady's, realizing for the first time, how dangerous it had all been.

Jolene opened her eyes the next morning to see sunshine spilling through a window onto her pillow. She was at the O'Gradys in the spare bedroom. What had happened last night flooded back to her, and her thoughts immediately went to Harp and Sean. Were they both alright? Had Harp found Sean?

Jolene climbed out of bed and slipped out of her borrowed nightgown. Pulling her clothes on, Jolene picked up a brush from the small washstand in the corner and quickly brushed and braided her long black hair. Tying the end of her braid with a piece of rawhide that had been in her pocket, Jolene left the room. Her bare feet made no sound at all as she went down the stairs.

Mrs. O'Grady was moving around the sunny little kitchen, pouring coffee and frying bacon. Her hair was done neatly and she had on a starched white apron. Her face was calm, as if nothing had happened the night before, and her son was not missing.

Jolene glanced around. There was no sign of O'Grady. "Where's Mr. O'Grady?" Jolene asked, still standing at the bottom of the stairs.

Mrs. O'Grady straightened up from where she had been bent over the stove. "Goodness, ye startled me!"

"I'm sorry."

"That's alright. Come an' sit." Mrs. O'Grady motioned to a kitchen chair. "Danny left fer work a few minutes ago." She sighed. "He wanted to go with Harp, but I'm afraid Danny wouldna make it with that bad leg o' his."

Jolene spent the day with Mrs. O'Grady–baking, dusting, anything to keep them busy. Mrs. O'Grady tried to act cheerful, but Jolene could tell it was forced. They were both worried.

When the sun began to sink slowly behind the mountain peaks, they waited anxiously for O'Grady to come home. He was a little late, but he arrived. Both women breathed a sigh of relief as he led his horse to the shed.

The supper table was quiet at first. Then, O'Grady spoke. "Been thinkin', Jolene. What do ye plan to do with yer life?"

Jolene stopped eating. "I don't know really. I might go back to my hometown…" Her voice trailed off. What *was* she going to do?

The O'Gradys shared a glance.

"We'd like ye to stay here with us," Mrs. O'Grady said softly. "If ye'd like. Ye would be of a help now with a baby on the way."

A baby! And they wanted her to stay! Jolene bit her lower lip. Of course she wanted to stay…But should she? Well, there was nothing left back home.

"Alright," she said finally. "I'll stay."

Both O'Grady's faces brightened considerably.

"Good!" O'Grady's voice was louder than he'd intended. "Ye'll have to write Elizabeth an' tell her."

Jolene nodded. The atmosphere was decidedly more cheerful after that. The next thing O'Grady said brought excitement to her heart. "I been thinkin' 'bout thet gold too. I been wantin' to start a horse ranch."

Jolene looked up, waiting for him to say more.

"There was a fella in town who brought in a band o' wild horses. He sold 'em cheap."

"*Sold?*" Mrs. O'Grady questioned. "Ye mean ye bought them?"

"Yeah." O'Grady looked sheepish. "Guess I did."

"Where are they now?"

"Fella in town's rentin' me a corral 'til I kin expand."

"An' how long will that be?" Mrs. O'Grady wasn't mad and Jolene thought she seemed to like the idea.

"Dunno. S'gonna start tomorra. Ya know we have all these big acres of land an' only one little house."

"Yes?" Mrs. O'Grady leaned forward.

"Well, I was gonna build some barns an' corrals, mebbe fence in our property an' when the horses are branded, let 'em run."

"Are you going to hire someone to help?" Jolene asked.

"Well, I can't really do it meself with me bad leg. Mebbe hire two or three men." He paused, thinking. "I'd like to have thet Reddick fella hired on as foreman." He glanced at Jolene. "Was he headed somewheres, lass?"

"No...he wasn't." Jolene remembered his cool words. "I was goin' nowhere."

"Good," O'Grady said. "I'd like to have 'im."

The next day passed uneventfully. O'Grady had laid out plans for the ranch, but hadn't yet started building. Mrs. O'Grady was becoming more worried about Sean, and Jolene found it hard to go to sleep at night.

Then, the next day, as Jolene was emptying dishwater over the side of the porch, she saw a rider coming slowly down the road. At first, for one hopeful heartbeat, Jolene thought it was Harp. But, then, as she studied the rider, she knew it was not. The man on the horse didn't have the broad shoulders and the easy way in the saddle as Harp did. And there was no little boy in front of him.

Jolene went back inside where Mrs. O'Grady had started kneading bread dough. "Somebody's comin'."

Mrs. O'Grady wiped her hands on her apron, and the two of them stepped out on the porch. A warm breeze blew wisps of hair around Jolene's face. The rider was turning in the path at the gate. He looked strangely familiar.

The man pulled the horse to a stop and dismounted. Pulling his hat off, he slapped it against his jeans to rid them of dust. As he raised his head, Jolene recognized him. It was Ben.

Flipping the horse's reins around the fence, Ben walked up the little walk that led to the house. He grinned as he saw them standing there. "Howdy, Mrs. O'Grady, Jolene."

"Hello, Ben," Mrs. O'Grady said pleasantly. "What brings ye here?"

"I left Kansas to come live in Colorado."

"Why?" Jolene asked curiously.

Ben shrugged. "I like the territory."

"Won't ye come in?" Mrs. O'Grady questioned, motioning toward the door to the kitchen.

"Believe I will."

The three went into the house and Mrs. O'Grady began getting lemonade and cookies. Ben eased into a kitchen chair and sighed. Putting his hat on the table he glanced at Jolene. "Got a letter fer ya. Picked it up goin' through yer hometown."

"Who's it from?" Jolene sat down in a chair, setting the plate of cookies on the table.

"Lizabeth." He said the nickname casually as he slid the letter across the table to Jolene.

Elizabeth? What would she be writing so soon for? Boredom? The address wasn't written in Elizabeth's usual neat script. Instead it was hurried and sloppy.

Frowning, Jolene opened the envelope. There was only one piece of paper inside. Unfolding it, Jolene quickly scanned it's contents.

Dear Jolene.

This is going to be short. Our wagon was caught in a flooded river and smashed to pieces. Aunt Sophie was hurt. Uncle Craig is taking her to the next fort along with the wagon train. He wants to get home to Oregon as soon as possible. We had an argument last night, which I won. We didn't get across the river—we're waiting for it to calm. When the wagon smashed, we swam back to the side we'd come from. There is a strange disease breaking out among the people in our train. I'm scared. I miss you and I'm coming back. Yes, coming back. There are a few people going back to Missouri. After all, we are only half way and they know what's behind and not what's ahead. They are scared and they are mostly old people and young single women. I will travel with them to Colorado. Don't ask how I won the argument with Uncle Craig. I just knew I had to go home. I had to get away from the wagon train. I couldn't be happy in Oregon. Uncle Craig is only a little angry. I'll see you hopefully soon.
Love, Elizabeth

Jolene carefully folded the letter and slipped it back in the envelope. When she looked up, she realized Ben and Mrs. O'Grady were looking at her questioningly. For the first time in a long time, Jolene smiled, and really meant it. "Elizabeth's coming back."

Before the words could even click in Mrs. O'Grady's or Ben's minds, there was the sound of a pistol shot. The dead silence that always seemed to follow the sound of a gun filled the morning air. Then, the silence was pierced by a yell.

The three in the kitchen stared at each other. Jolene looked at Mrs. O'Grady and saw in the woman's eyes, the same question she was thinking. What would happen now?

CHAPTER SEVENTEEN

Jolene was first to regain her senses. Getting up, she went over to a window and peered out. Ben followed, looking over her shoulder.

Outside, there were two horses besides Ben's. One was riderless. O'Grady was holstering a pistol and hobbling toward the house, yelling for Meagan and whooping.

Jolene's eyes traveled to a tall broad shouldered figure swinging a little boy down from a gray gelding. Harp!

"They're back!" Jolene's bare feet hardly touched the boards as she flew out the door, followed by Mrs. O'Grady and a confused Ben.

O'Grady grabbed Mrs. O'Grady as she came out the door. "He found 'im, Meagan. He found 'im!" He started whirling her around.

Jolene stopped on the first step, unsure of what to do. Harp and Sean were coming toward them. Sean was fairly clean and his face was split with a huge smile.

As usual, Jolene couldn't see Harp's face for the hat that was pulled down low. His shirt was so stained with dirt and dried blood that Jolene couldn't even tell what color it had been.

Mrs. O'Grady had managed to free herself and now Sean was running toward her.

Harp stopped and watched Sean get swept into loving arms. Then Harp's gaze went to Jolene. She was standing on the top step, watching him. Not Sean, not the O'Gradys, but him.

There was a movement behind Jolene, and Harp saw a young man standing there with a bewildered look on his face. A sudden disliking rose up in Harp. Who was that man an' what was he doin' here? He didn't look like the sort of man who would be doing a lot of hard work or riding. Kinda scrawny lookin'.

Harp shifted his gaze back to Jolene and started for the porch. She looked right pretty standing there.

Her eyes were on him the whole way. Slowly, he went up the steps. She had to look up to meet his blue eyes. "So, you made it," she said softly.

He grinned. "Guess so. Glad?"

A smile broke over her face. "Yes."

He put an arm around her shoulders and pulled her to him for a second. Her hair smelled good. He felt her lean her head against his chest and his pulse throbbed. Then, over her head, his eyes met those of the young man behind her. There was surprise written in them.

Gently, Harp released Jolene, his eyes still locked with those of the young man.

Jolene, her heart still beating fast, stepped back, knowing her cheeks were flushed.

The O'Gradys were coming up the porch. Harp's eyes were still locked with Ben's. Jolene felt the tension.

Ben looked away first, darting a glance down at Harp's boots, then up again. Clearing his throat, he spoke. "Howdy, stranger."

"Howdy, *stranger*." Harp's voice emphasized the last word. His thumbs were hooked on his gunbelts.

Ben shifted his feet and stuck out his hand, beginning to get nervous. "Ben Wheatstalk."

"Harp Reddick." Harp's hand met Ben's with an iron grip and squeezed. Ben grimaced, his eyes widening as he swallowed hard.

Jolene saw a smile touch the corners of Harp's mouth. "Ah, hope I didn' hurt you."

Ben withdrew his limp hand. "No, uh, you didn't." Jolene saw him discreetly wiggle his fingers.

"Well," O'Grady said, sounding amused, "Guess we could go inside an' Harp could tell us how he so happened ta get Sean."

"Sure."

They filed into the house, Sean holding his mother's hand tightly.

There were just enough chairs at the kitchen table for all of them. Mrs. O'Grady and Jolene began to get lunch ready as Harp began to tell his story.

"Well," he said, leaning back in his chair, his eyes roaming the room. "I'll make it brief. I followed the trail for a while an' it wasn't long afore the fella cut into a stream. Sort of a precaution I guess. Took me all night to finally figger out where they'd cut back onto land.

"Bout mid-mornin' I came to the top of a rise an' saw smoke from a campfire. Guess the fella had no idea he was bein' followed so he decided to rest. Guess he weren't the brilliant type neither. He sent the boy down to a stream to fill their canteens. That's where I grabbed the kid an' put 'im on the horse an' rode up to the fella. He pulled his gun."

Harp paused, his eyes following Jolene as she carried a plate of sandwiches to the table.

"Well?" Ben asked.

Harp looked at him, as if surprised to see him sitting there. "Well, I shot 'im."

There was a silence.

"How's your arm?" Jolene asked as she set out plates.

"Purty good. Put some herbs on it an' some whiskey. Bandaged it." His eyes were on the food.

O'Grady chuckled. "Ye been eyein' that food ever since we got in. How long since ye last ate?"

"Two days. Fed what food I had to the boy. Didn't really have time to stop an' hunt."

"Two days!" Mrs. O'Grady exclaimed. "Why, ye must be starved!"

"Yes, ma'am."

It proved to be true because Jolene lost track of Harp's helpings after he reached four—and she was still on her first.

"Mighty good, ma'am," Harp said, letting his fork fall to his plate. "Best food I had in months."

Mrs. O'Grady smiled. "Thank you, Harp."

"Welcome."

As the two women began clearing dishes, O'Grady cleared his throat. "Harp, I been thinkin'."

Harp looked at him. "What about?"

"Well, I figgered the only way I could git all that gold off my hands was to spend it. I'm goin' to start a horse ranch."

Harp's blue eyes fastened intently on O'Grady and Jolene saw the flash of interest in them as O'Grady said the words, "horse ranch."

"So," O'Grady said, abruptly changing the subject. "Ye plannin' on goin' anywheres soon?"

"Not that I know of. Just gonna git a job."

"Ye found one!" O'Grady said triumphantly.

Harp raised an eyebrow. "I have?"

"Yep. I'd like to hire ye on as foreman of the ranch. I need an honest hard worker. As long as ye agree, the job's yers."

Harp leaned back in his chair, seeming to think it over.

Now that the dishes were done, Jolene sat down in her chair again and brushed a strand of hair back. Mrs. O'Grady took her seat beside Mr. O'Grady. All three waited in suspense for his answer.

"Ye'd get good pay," O'Grady said. Then added, "Jolene's stayin' too."

Harp let his eyes rest on Jolene. He could see they all wanted him to stay. He looked at O'Grady. "Well..."

They held their breath.

He grinned. "You got yerself a deal."

O'Grady let out a sigh of relief. "Now all we need is maybe one more man..." Suddenly his eyes lit on Ben. "You willin'?"

Ben looked surprised. "Yes, sir. Sure as anythin'."

O'Grady gave a smile of satisfaction. "I'm a happy man."

"About to get happier," Mrs. O'Grady said, winking at Jolene. "Elizabeth's on her way back."

O'Grady's mouth dropped open. "Well, I'll be."

Jolene smiled. Life had made a complete turnabout. Everything was coming out happy instead of sad. Nearly all of her troubles and bothers had disappeared. The only thing to mar her happiness was the deep ache that came from missing her family, and even that wasn't so bad as it used to be.

Then, she noticed Ben and Harp eyeing one another again. Ben's gaze was cold, almost a glare. Harps eyes were like blue fire, yet cool as ice.

Why were they acting this way, Jolene wondered. It seemed to be hate at first sight. Or was it first sight?

CHAPTER EIGHTEEN

Jolene soon found out that O'Grady had quit his job in town and bought more land. It was after supper and Harp, Mr. O'Grady, and Ben were huddled around the kitchen table. Harp was sketching with a stub of a pencil on a scrap of paper, while O'Grady and Ben watched intently. They were making plans for the barns and it seemed that O'Grady had never done it, Ben had a slightly better idea of how to do it, and Harp had helped build several.

Sean had fallen asleep on the floor in front of the fireplace and the two women were clearing what was left on the table.

Jolene reached around Harp for a plate, and as he shifted to make room, she caught the scent of soap. He had gotten a bath and shaved, and even changed his shirt. He was the cleanest Jolene had ever seen him. His scar stood out even more on his jaw and his hair was still damp.

He's better looking than I thought, Jolene thought suddenly. Then, she quickly pushed the thoughts aside and began stacking the rest of the plates.

As usual, after the supper dishes were done, Jolene slipped out the door and made her way to the small corral where the horses were kept. She missed having horses around all the time, and she surely couldn't wait until O'Grady and Harp got the ranch built. And of course Ben would help.

Jolene stepped up onto the bottom rail of the fence and watched the horses standing lazily in the sinking sunlight, their tails swishing flies.

Jolene took a deep breath, inhaling the good smell of horses and sun dried grass. It was nearing summer and was already starting to get hot in the afternoons.

Harps tall gray gelding ambled over to her and Jolene rubbed her hand over its velvety nose. The horse stepped forward, nearly pushing her off the fence. With a nicker, the horse tossed its head, his eyes fastened on something over Jolene's shoulder.

Jolene turned to see Harp step up behind her and reach out a hand to stroke the horse's neck. Jolene wanted to know why he'd been mad at Ben, but she kept her mouth shut.

Harp spoke. "What made ya decide to stay here?"

"I don't know." Jolene watched as the gray turned and trotted around the corral. "I didn't have any other place to go and not a cent to my name." She paused. "What about you? Don't you have any family?"

Harp pushed his hat back, his face expressionless. "Nope. We lived in Utah. My parents died when I was four, leaving my only brother to take care of me. He was fourteen. For a while, we just stayed in town. He worked an' we rented a hotel room.

"That went on until I was old enough to work. Then we traveled further west. We worked a sheep ranch for a while. Til the war. My brother went to fight, told me to stay home. Few months later, he died. The ranch went to pieces an' I lived with the Utes fer a while. Then I made up my mind to fight an' went to war.

"When I got back from the war, I left Utah. Never goin' back neither." He looked at her. "I told you my life, you tell me yers."

Jolene did, using the same briefness he had. By the time she'd finished, it was nearly dark.

They turned to go back to the porch, and Jolene was surprised to see Ben and the O'Gradys sitting on the porch. Ben was talking animatedly, waving his hands around to explain things.

Jolene glanced at Harp. He was frowning and seemed to be deep in thought.

It was dark when O'Grady finally announced that they should get to bed. "Hope you fellas don't mind sleepin' in the shed. There's plenty o' straw an' extry blankets."

"I'll live," Ben said, grinning.

Harp gave a nod. "I've slept a lot worse places 'n a horse shed."

O'Grady nodded. "Okay, then. Don' kill each other." The last part he said teasingly, but his eyes were serious.

"Try not to," Harp said in a low voice, and went down the porch steps into the darkness.

Ben gave a shrug and followed Harp, tossing a good night over his shoulder.

By the time Ben reached the shed, Harp had lit a lantern and laid out his bedroll. Ben took out his own bedroll from his saddle which was hanging over a sawhorse, and laid it a careful distance from Harp. Sitting down, Ben began taking off his boots, keeping a wary eye on Harp.

Harp stripped off his shirt and began unwrapping a bandage from his shoulder.

Ben gulped. If one of them was going to get killed, it surely wasn't going to be Harp. The man was solid muscle and on his feet, he moved like an Indian. Ben watched him examine the wound, then struggle to one-handedly re-wrap the bloody bandage.

"Need help?" the words were out before Ben could stop them.

Harp looked up and deliberately met his gaze. "Nope."

Tension was thick. Ben bristled. What was wrong with this man anyway?

"Would you mind tellin' me why you took such a dislikin' to my company?" Ben's voice was cool.

Surprise registered in Harp's eyes. "You don' know?"

"No! How could I know when I just first laid eyes on you today?"

Harp let out a deep breath and rubbed the back of his neck. Well, Ben had a point there. "You related to Paul Ivan Wheatstalk?"

Ben scowled. "No. Never heard of him."

Harp's eyes narrowed. "You sure?"

"Sure I'm sure!"

Harp relaxed a bit. Ben was telling the truth. Could tell by his eyes and the way he said it. "Guess I'll explain a bit. When I was fifteen, I worked a sheep ranch in Utah. Had some trouble with two men—Ben and Paul Wheatstalk. They killed one of my friends. When I heard your name, I guess I sorta jumped to conclusions."

"Guess you did."

Harp's face darkened. "Look, do you wanna cause trouble? Cause I will."

Ben shook his head. "Sorry."

"You'd better be."

Harp laid down and flipped his blanket over himself. "G'night."

"G'night," Ben muttered and reached over to put out the lantern, then paused. "Harp, you mind tellin' me what happened to this Paul Wheatstalk?"

"He's dead."

Ben thought for minute, nodded, and put out the lantern.

Ben opened his eyes to see Harp sitting propped up against the stall wall, cleaning one of his guns. Groggily, Ben sat up. "You always carry them hoglegs?"

"Yep. Since I was fifteen."

"You fast?"

Harp paused and glanced at him, then continued cleaning. "Purty fast."

Ben grinned. "Yer whoppin' it."

Harp's head snapped up, his eyes angry.

"I mean," Ben quickly went on, "I heard talk of you as one of the fastest gunhawks in this territory."

Harp relaxed and went back to continue cleaning his gun.

Ben stifled a groan. What would it take for Harp to not act as if he wasn't doing a favor, just by not killing him?

Jolene noticed at breakfast that Ben and Harp weren't so tense. She took that as a good sign. That and the fact that Harp hadn't killed Ben. She knew Ben wouldn't harm anyone unless absolutely necessary and even then, she wasn't sure how he was at defending himself.

That morning, the three men left to take a look around the property and where would be best for corrals and fences.

It wasn't long after they left that there were two riders coming through the gate.

Sean, who had been playing with some scraps of wood in the yard came flying in. "Ma, somebody's comin'!"

Jolene and Mrs. O'Grady went to the door. The horses were lathered with dust and sweat. The men on top were wearing long overcoats. "Hello, ladies," one said, touching his hat brim.

Jolene felt uneasy. What were these men here for? Her mind flashed back to the time, only a matter of months before, when a rider had come to her home. She'd had the same feeling. Something was wrong.

The man shifted in his saddle and let his eyes roam the small stead. He finally looked back at them and his gaze rested on Jolene. "S'ere a man around here by the name of Harp Reddick?"

Mrs. O'Grady started to speak, but Jolene touched her hand, silencing her.

The man caught the movement. "Where is 'e?" He tightened the reins, causing his horse to dance in place.

Jolene stepped forward, clasping her hands nervously in front of her. Her voice came out strong and clear. "What do you want with him?"

"Well, miss." The man seemed to be sizing her up as he ran his eyes over her. "He's wanted for murder."

CHAPTER NINETEEN

"Y̶ou're wrong," Jolene stated flatly. "Harp's not the murderin' type."
The man's face remained calm. "Well then, he's the type to kill a man
without reason."

Jolene glared at him. "No."

"Yes." The man smiled. "You might as well just tell us where he is. We'll
find him sooner or later."

This time Sean answered. "You can't take Harp! He's my friend!" The
little boy stood on the porch, his arms crossed and a fierce look on his face.

Both men laughed. "Well," said the taller one who had been doing the
talking. "We might as well get down an' have a look around."

Jolene saw Mrs. O'Grady pull Sean closer.

The men dismounted, ground tying their horses. They came up on the
porch now and stopped, both looking at Jolene. She glared back at them, her
hands still clasped in front of her, her shoulders straight and her back rigid.

The shorter man reached out and touched a strand of glossy hair that had
escaped from Jolene's braid. Jolene didn't flinch.

"Hey, Mike," the man said, flashing a grin. "This girl sure is purty."

Mrs. O'Grady stepped forward, her voice filled with quiet anger. "Ye'll
do well not to lay a hand on that girl."

The short one laughed and was about to strike Mrs. O'Grady when the tall
one stopped him. "We come after Reddick, not after women."

Reluctantly, the short one stepped back and the tall one glanced at the two
women. "If Harp's inside, you'd better bring him out." This time there was no
mocking politeness about him. He meant it.

"He's not in there," Mrs. O'Grady said quietly, holding Sean's hand
tightly.

"Well, where is he?" The man was almost yelling.

Mrs. O'Grady went pale and glanced at Jolene. Jolene would not meet her
eyes. She was not going to tell if they killed her. Only if they threatened Sean
or Mrs. O'Grady would she so much as say a word to these men.

"He left," Mrs. O'Grady said quietly. "This morning he went out with my husband and a friend."

"Which way?"

Mrs. O'Grady looked at Jolene, a sudden glint in her eye. "They went that way." Mrs. O'Grady pointed. Jolene looked. It was the exact opposite direction in which they had gone.

The tall man's eyes narrowed. "You lyin' to me, ma'am?"

"Why would I lie to ye?" Mrs. O'Grady asked serenely. "As ye said, ye're goin' to find him sooner or later."

The man smiled. "You're right about that, ma'am, you're right about that." He turned to the other man. "Shorty, we're headin' out."

Jolene and Mrs. O'Grady watched the men mount. The tall one tipped his hat. "Thank you, ladies."

They kicked their horses into a trot and left the yard.

As soon as they were out of sight, Jolene looked at Mrs. O'Grady. "Isn't that the way Harp will be coming back?"

Mrs. O'Grady chuckled and shook her head. "No, they're comin' back further east. Those men headed due west. Harp 'n' O'Grady 'n' Ben'll be back afore they figger out what's goin' on."

They went inside again, but couldn't relax. They were all waiting for the trio to make it back unharmed.

They hadn't waited but an hour when Jolene heard deep voices on the porch. Harp's and O'Grady's voices. And Ben's.

Getting up from where she had been sorting scraps of cloth for quilt piecing, Jolene hurried to the door and unbarred it.

O'Grady's face looked surprised when she unbarred the door. "What's it barred fer?" he asked as he stepped inside.

"We had some visitors." Mrs. O'Grady arose from her kitchen chair to greet them.

"Thet's what Harp said when he saw the tracks." O'Grady looked around. "Who were they?"

Jolene watched Harp's face carefully as Mrs. O'Grady answered. "Two men lookin' fer Harp."

Harp frowned. It had to be trouble. "Who an' why?" His words came out gruffer than he'd intended.

Mrs. O'Grady hesitated. "They called each other Mike and Shorty."

The frown didn't leave Harp's face. "Don' know 'em. Why were they here?"

"They said you were a murderer," Sean spoke up from under the table where he'd been playing. "They were gonna take you away an' I told 'em they couldn't cause you were my friend an' they laughed." Sean paused for breath, his brow furrowing. "What's a murderer?"

There was dead silence in the room.

Harp broke it. "I'll tell you Sean. A murderer is something I'm not."

Sean smiled, unaware of the tension in the room. "Good. Jolene said you weren't. She was mad at them men. I think them men are murderers."

Harp looked at Jolene, his face unreadable. "Where'd they go?"

"Mrs. O'Grady sent them west," Jolene answered. "But that was an hour ago. They'll be back."

Harp turned and started for the door. Ben caught his arm. "Don't be a fool, Harp. It'd be best—" his voice broke off as he looked up.

Harp looked down at him. "Let go," he growled. "Who you callin' a fool? You don't know what's best for me. As for you—"

O'Grady broke in. "Harp!" His voice was sharp. "It'd be foolish to go after those men by yourself. Maybe—"

Harp interrupted. "Seems to me, this is my problem, not yours. You can't stop me, so don't try." This was the angriest Jolene had ever seen Harp. For a second she thought he was going to hit Ben.

Then Harp turned again and yanked open the door, rattling its hinges.

"Harp," came a small voice from under the table.

Slowly, struggling to control his temper, Harp turned around. Sean was peering around a chair. "Can I go with you?"

"No!" Harp went out and slammed the door.

Jolene flinched. Sean's lower lip quivered and he crawled out from under the table to run to his mother. They all listened to the sound of Harp's boots crossing the porch and going down the steps.

"Ma," Sean tugged his mother's skirt. "Why couldn't I go with Harp? I could sit behind him on his gray horse."

Mrs. O'Grady ruffled her son's hair. "It's too dangerous, honey. Ye could get hurt."

"Will Harp get hurt?"

Mrs. O'Grady sighed and looked at Jolene. "I hope not, Sean. I sure hope not."

They sat down at the table and Jolene and Mrs. O'Grady began getting lunch together. As she got out plates, Jolene could hear the horses whinnying in the corral.

Glancing out the window. Jolene saw Harp swing up on his mount. He was stubborn, too stubborn. Oh, why wouldn't he accept help?

Then, Jolene heard hoofbeats and nearly dropped the stack of plates.

Through the window, she could see Mike and Shorty riding out of the trees. And they didn't look too happy.

CHAPTER TWENTY

Harp sat on his horse, watching the riders coming in. Well, he'd tried to bring the gunfight away from the house. *I shoulda left as soon as I heard about 'em,* Harp thought. *If only that fool Wheatstalk hadna grabbed my arm...*

Well, it was too late now. The riders saw Harp as soon as they came out of the trees. When they were within twenty feet of him, they pulled their horses to a stop.

"Harp Reddick!" the tall one said, leveling a rifle at him. "Get off your horse!"

Slowly and deliberately, Harp swung down and stood beside his horse. "You fellas want somethin'?"

"You bet we do! You're a murderin'—" He broke off suddenly. Down the road was a wagon. It was nearing the house.

As both men's attentions were diverted, Harp covered ground with amazing speed and yanked the rifle out of the man's hand.

By this time, everyone in the house had gathered at the window. As Harp threw the rifle behind him, O'Grady started for the door. "He'll need help." He opened the door just in time to see Shorty reach for his gun.

Shorty reached before Harp, but Harp's was spitting flame before Shorty's had even cleared leather. Shorty gasped and clutched at his chest. Blood spurted from between his fingers. Then he fell from his horse, hitting the ground hard.

Mike started to reach for his gun, but Harp turned on him, his eyes glinting dangerously. "You so much as touch that gun, an' I'll shoot first an' talk afterwards. An' that might be a little hard on you, if you get the drift."

Mike eased his hand away from his gun.

"Get down from yer horse." Harp motioned with his gun. Reluctantly, Mike did so.

The wagon was rolling into the yard.

"Take off yer gunbelt," Harp growled, now aware of his audience. "An' be quick!"

Mike did, a cool smile touching his lips. "They didn' tell me you were this good, Reddick."

"You prob'ly didn' ask."

The smile vanished.

O'Grady moved onto the porch, his eyes on the wagon. "Elizabeth, thet you, lass?"

"I-It's me." Elizabeth looked scared, sitting beside an old man on the wagon seat. "Is it safe to get down?"

Harp didn't glance at her as he spoke. "You kin get down. Just hurry up."

Elizabeth slid down from the wagon seat, clutching a satchel to her chest, and nearly ran to O'Grady.

The man who'd been driving, and who Harp supposed was deaf and half-blind, turned the wagon out of the yard and down the road.

"Now," Harp said, running his eyes over the man before him as if sizing him up for a fight. "What were you sayin' about murder?"

"Well," Mike shifted. "You murdered my brother back in Utah."

Harp raised an eyebrow. "Who was yer brother?"

"Eustace Bromwell. We had us a sheep ranch back of yours. When he went to talk with you about a sheep that'd been killed by a dog, you mur—" Mike stopped mid-sentence at the look on Harp's face.

"I shot your brother," Harp's voice was calmer than he looked. "But I didn't murder him. He drew his gun first."

"He didn't have a chance. He was half drunk an' you knew it."

"I know he was half drunk. An' he was standin' two feet away when he grabbed for his gun."

"You shot him." Mike's voice was low as if he knew he had lost the argument.

"It's called self-defense," Harp said dryly.

Mike ran a hand over his face. "The only brothers I ever had, you shot."

"Ain't my fault. They seemed to have itchy trigger fingers."

Mike shook his head. "It's useless," he muttered. "Useless."

Harp watched him in silence.

"What're you gonna do with me?" Mike asked, raising his head. "Shoot me?"

"I don't shoot unarmed men." Harp paused, thinking, then motioned for Mike to pick up his gunbelt. "I'm tellin' you to leave an' not come back. If you do, I *will* shoot you."

Hastily, Mike buckled his gunbelts. Keeping an eye on Harp, Mike eased over to Shorty and hoisted the dead body over the saddle of his horse. Then, he mounted his own horse. For a second, his hand hovered over his gun as he looked down at Harp. Then, he rested both hands on the pommel of the saddle. "I'll never understand you."

"Good. Don't try." Harp holstered his gun. "Now git!"

Mike kicked the horse into a trot, and leading Shorty's horse, he left the yard.

Harp watched them leave, then he took the reins of the gelding and led it back toward the shed.

Everyone inside was holding their breath as they watched Mike ride away. As Harp led his horse toward the barn, they all moved back from the window.

Jolene was the first one in Elizabeth's arms. Then Mrs. O'Grady. Then Sean. Ben moved in next and Jolene saw Elizabeth hesitate, then give him a hug.

The embraces had just stopped when Harp came in the open door. Every eye in the room was on him.

He took off his hat and nodded at Elizabeth. "Sorry 'bout the welcome, miss. Weren't supposed to happen that way."

There was a low ripple of laughter and the tension broke. "That's okay," Elizabeth said, "As long as you're on our side."

More laughter.

Harp glanced around. "Guess I should sorta apologize about this mess. If I hadna been here, this wouldna happened."

"Nonsense!" Mrs. O'Grady moved forward. "Everyone's alive an' well an' that's all that matters."

Harp gave a nod, but Jolene could tell he still felt bad.

Mr. O'Grady moved forward. "Harp, this is Jolene's sister, Elizabeth. Elizabeth, this here's our friend Harp Reddick."

Elizabeth gave a sweet smile but Harp only managed a stiff nod.

"Well," Mrs. O'Grady said. "Why don't you all sit down while I start lunch. It'll take a while an' I'm sure ye have much to catch up on."

"Oh, yes!" Elizabeth exclaimed. "Let's!"

Ben laughed at her and she stuck out her tongue.

They sat down at the table and O'Grady started telling the story of the two men in the snakeskin boots. As Jolene listened, she noticed that Harp seemed restless. It wasn't long before he excused himself and left the room. Jolene could see his tall figure through the window, striding toward the barns. Jolene couldn't help wondering what was bothering him. Then, when Ben was telling an animated story about back in Kansas, Jolene slipped out of the room. As she went down the porch steps, she could hear Elizabeth's laughter rippling through the window.

At the bottom Jolene paused. Harp was nowhere in sight. Jolene headed for the shed where Ben and Harp slept. He would surely be in there.

CHAPTER TWENTY-ONE

He was. He was sitting on the straw with his back propped against the wall, cleaning his gun. His head snapped up as Jolene entered.

"You're jumpy," she said. "Mind if I sit down?" For a minute, she remembered how she used to always be unsure around him. She wasn't sure when, but he'd gained her trust.

"Go 'head." He motioned with his head toward the straw.

Jolene took a seat on the straw, carefully smoothing her skirts down over her knees. She watched his hands take the gun apart, carefully setting the cylinder aside. She marveled at the way he did it so methodically, as if he wasn't even thinking about it.

Well, Jolene thought, *guess I'd better start askin' if I ever want to get some answers.*

"Harp," she began.

"What?" He didn't even look up as he rubbed a grease rag over the barrel.

"Is that your real name?" she asked, suddenly curious, though it wasn't the question she'd intended to ask.

"Nope. I was baptized Curt Reddick. Called Harp because I used to play the mouth harp so much. Soon ever'body was callin' me Harp."

"Do you still play?"

"Sometimes. When I git lonely."

Jolene decided to get back on track. "Harp," she started again.

"What?" He slid the cylinder back in.

"Are you mad at Ben?"

"Why'd ya say that?"

"You don't seem to like him very much."

Harp looked at her, his eyes twinkling. "I don't."

His good humor, combined with his good looks took Jolene off guard and she had to smile.

He grinned before giving the gun a final rub with the rag. "To tell you the truth, he gets on my nerves a bit. He doesn't think before he does. Guess he'll learn. He's not bad."

Harp looked at Jolene, a sudden suspicion gnawing at his insides. "Does it bother you when I act a little stiff around him?"

Jolene nodded.

"You like 'im?"

Jolene looked up, startled. Harp's face was unreadable as he gazed back. "No. What ever gave you that idea?"

"You did." Harp turned the gun over and examined it, though Jolene could see not a smudge or a speck of dirt on it.

"Well," Jolene said, "I don't. Elizabeth likes him. And anyway, he's not my type."

"What is your type?" Harp stopped examining the gun to look her straight in the eye.

Jolene felt herself blushing. "Well, not him."

"Ya know," Harp said, shoving his gun into its holster and pulling a wicked looking knife out of his boot, "you an' yer sister aren't anything alike."

"I know," Jolene rearranged her skirts. "That's what everybody says."

"She's a lot more talkative than you are."

A sudden impulse came upon Jolene. "You like her?"

Harp's head snapped up, surprised. Then he saw the teasing in her eyes. "No," he drawled. "Whatever gave you that idea?"

Jolene fought against a smile. "You did."

"Well," Harp said, his eyes laughing. "I don't. Ben likes her, an' anyway, she's not my type."

"What is?"

Their eyes met and they started laughing. Harp had to stop polishing the knife so he wouldn't cut himself.

Then they heard the bell that Mrs. O'Grady kept for calling Sean to the house when he was playing in the yard.

Harp tucked the knife back into his boot and stood up. "Let's go eat."

He reached down a hand and helped Jolene up. She brushed the straw from her skirts and they started for the house.

Harp was whistling when they headed across the yard.

They went inside the house and for a second, Jolene was afraid Harp was going to turn back to his usual sober self.

But after a tug at Jolene's braid, Harp took off his hat and took a seat beside Ben.

Jolene helped bring on the rest of the food. When they sat down to eat, Jolene noticed that Harp joined in the conversation willingly. She also noticed that his eyes didn't turn cold when Ben to spoke to him or Jolene. She hadn't noticed how withdrawn he'd been until now. The only thing was, she wondered why.

After super, Jolene again went to the corral. The gray came over again. This time Jolene was ready when he pushed his velvet nose past her. She'd expected Harp to follow.

"Howdy, Lena." He paused. "Mind if I call you that?"

Jolene shook her head. "I like it. The only person who called me that was Uncle Craig. And he lives in Oregon."

Harp nodded, his eyes on the horses. "Can't wait to start buildin'. It's like I'm startin' life all over again. All fresh an' new with no mistakes."

Jolene didn't want to ruin it, but suddenly she had to know. "Harp, if you don't mind my askin', what put you in such a good mood?"

Harp grinned and fastened his blue eyes on her. "Thought you might ask that. Well, I just decided I couldn't spend the rest of my life livin' from my mistakes an' feelin' bad when I done somethin' wrong. Gotta learn to forget the bad things and look fer the good things."

"What made you decide that?" Jolene was surprised at the reasons he'd given.

"You did."

"I did?" Jolene was startled. What had *she* done...

"Yep." Harp rested his hands on the fence. "I was thinkin' about it before you came to the barn. You always seemed willin' to forgive an' forget. Decided I'd try it."

Jolene felt his hand, strong and calloused, close over top of hers on the fence rail. "An' I believe I like it."

The next few months went quickly for Jolene. The ranch was built, the horses branded and let loose, and more horses were bought.

Jolene began to notice a friendship beginning to bond between Harp and Ben. They both worked hard, side by side.

Harp had surprised Jolene. By his mood and also by the way he threw himself into ranching. Jolene could tell he loved it. He loved the horses, the hard labor, and even the thick layers of dust that covered him by the end of each day.

Jolene herself loved the ranch. Everyone did, but Jolene more so. It was almost like old times with her family. Except Harp was there. Jolene tried not to think about it much, but she knew their friendship was turning into more than friendship.

It was one day in late December when Mrs. O'Grady rang the bell. The morning was slowly moving on to mid-day and there was a dusting of powdery snow on the ground. The clouds in the sky were gray with an upcoming storm.

Jolene knew something was wrong when she heard the clanging . O'Grady and Ben were cleaning a few stalls while Jolene and Harp fed and watered the horses.

All four stopped what they were doing and ran for the house. But it wasn't Mrs. O'Grady ringing the bell. It was Elizabeth. Her face was pale and she had Sean by the hand.

Jolene felt an odd feeling curl in the pit of her stomach. She recognized it as fear.

"What is it?" O'Grady panted, skidding to a halt on his gimp leg.

Sean spoke up, in a small voice that seemed to echo over the quiet stillness of the yard. "Ma said she's gonna have the baby now."

CHAPTER TWENTY-TWO

O'Grady's face turned as gray as the sky. For a second no one spoke, their breath making puffs of vapor in the cold morning air. A large fluffy snowflake fell from the sky. Then another followed. Then another.

"A baby?" Ben asked, as if in a stupor. "I didn't even know she was…" his voice trailed off.

"What'd you think—she was just gaining weight?" Harp snapped. Jolene saw the flash of his old mood and dislike for Ben.

O'Grady came out of his trance and pushed past them, hobbling as fast as he could go. Elizabeth and Sean followed.

Flakes were falling fast and thick and the wind was picking up.

Elizabeth appeared at the door in a second. "A doctor—"

"I'm goin'." Harp sprinted for the barn. Within seconds, Jolene saw him through the snowflakes. On the back of the gray gelding, they were galloping toward the road. The horse had not one inch of tack on. Not even a halter.

It had all happened within seconds; Elizabeth ringing the bell and Harp riding off.

"What are we going to do now?" Ben asked, looking at Jolene.

"Go back and finish cleaning the stalls." Jolene could hardly see the barns for the snow that was falling. "I'm going inside to see if there's anything I can do."

Ben nodded and started toward the barn.

"If the snow gets any worse," Jolene yelled after him, "Come back to the house!"

His reply was lost in the wind.

Jolene went inside. Elizabeth was standing in the middle of the kitchen, chewing her bottom lip, her blue-gray eyes large with uncertainty.

"Why don't you get your coat and boots and go help Ben in the barn." Jolene asked gently. Her sister nodded and went for her coat.

Jolene cautiously entered the open bedroom. Mrs. O'Grady lay in bed covered by a blanket. Her stomach made a small hill in the covers.

Mr. O'Grady and Sean stood by her bedside. They turned as Jolene entered, still wearing her jacket.

Jolene noticed Mrs. O'Grady looked calm compared to Mr. O'Grady.

"A doctor—" Mr. O'Grady said.

"Harp's gone," Jolene answered.

"In this storm?" Mrs. O'Grady looked out the window. "I hope he's careful. Ye can barely see out there."

Jolene had thought of that, but she had seen no other choice. She couldn't have stopped him if she'd tried, anyway.

"Jolene," Mr. O'Grady asked abruptly. "Do ye know anythin' about birthin' babies?"

Jolene hesitated. Not really. "I've only ever helped with horses.." her voice trailed off.

"That's alright," Mrs. O'Grady said. "The baby's comin' but it'll be a while afore it's here. The doctor'll probly be here."

It was a few hours later, with snow falling fast and thick, wind picking up, and no sign of Harp or the doctor, when Mrs. O'Grady first cried out. Jolene, Elizabeth, Ben, and Sean were in the sitting room, gathered around the fireplace. They all jumped at the sound.

Jolene heard the low rumble of O'Grady's voice as he said something.

The next thing they knew, O'Grady came to the door of the sitting room. "Jolene," he began nervously.

Someone pounded on the front door. All five headed for kitchen, all of them hoping for the doctor.

Jolene opened the door. Doc Miller entered, holding his little black medical bag and wearing a heavy coat that nearly reached the floor, a wool cap, heavy mittens, and a scarf.

Unwrapping his scarf, he exclaimed, "Ghastly weather! Not fit for man or beast!"

As O'Grady hurried to help the doctor take off his coat, Jolene noticed Harp wasn't there.

"Where's Harp?" She asked anxiously.

"Is that the tall gun-slingin' fella who fetched me? Think he said he was gonna care fer the horses."

Once unwrapped, Jolene could see the doctor was a thin older man with bushy gray sideburns and dark eyes.

Doc Miller and O'Grady disappeared into the bedroom, shutting the door. The other four sat down at the kitchen table. Sean crawled into Jolene's lap. "Where's Harp? Did he get lost in the snow?"

"No," Jolene said, pulling the little boy close. "He's just putting the horses away."

The words were no sooner out of her mouth when the door opened again, the wind blowing cold air and snow into the warm kitchen.

Harp leaned back against the door to close it "Did we make it?" The words were spoken through lips numb with cold.

"You made it just in time." Jolene set Sean off her lap. "Elizabeth get some cups while I start making coffee."

Elizabeth stood. "Ben get some more wood on the fire. Harp needs to thaw out." Humbly, Ben got up and went to the woodbox in the corner.

Jolene set the coffee on to boil and turned to see Harp fumbling with the buttons on his coat. His fingers were so stiff, he couldn't grasp the buttons.

Going over to him, Jolene began nimbly unbuttoning his coat. "You should wear something on your hands, Harp."

"Don't need to."

She opened her mouth to reply but he cut in. "You don't wear anything on your hands, so I wouldn' talk if I was you."

He was right. As she continued unbuttoning his coat, she could feel him studying her. She felt herself blushing under his close scrutiny. She dared not look up because she knew, if she did, she would be staring directly into his blue eyes.

She stepped back, finished with the buttons.

Harp pulled the coat off and then his boots. Taking off his hat, he hung it on a peg near the door and took a seat in a kitchen chair. Sean appeared at his elbow and began asking him questions about his ride.

Jolene couldn't hear a sound from the bedroom. Was that good or bad?

Jolene jerked awake. She'd fallen asleep curled up in the cushioned rocking chair in the sitting room. Glancing around the room, she saw that the fire was still crackling in the fireplace. The clock on the mantel above the hearth said twelve. Midnight.

Elizabeth had gone upstairs to bed at ten. Jolene had stayed downstairs in case O'Grady called. Harp and Ben had stayed inside also, for the snow was too thick to see the bunkhouse, or even the yard for that matter.

Now Ben lay on the couch, his face buried in one of Mrs. O'Grady's pillows that were always kept on couch. He had the spare blanket that Jolene had fetched for him wrapped tightly around him like a cocoon.

Harp was sprawled on the love seat, his long legs stretched out in front of him on the floor, his blanket still folded neatly and sitting on the floor where Jolene had left it.

Jolene listened, but all she could hear was the fire and deep breathing. What had awakened her?

Then, O'Grady appeared in the doorway. When he saw Jolene was awake, a broad grin split his face. He motioned for her to follow and left the doorway.

Jolene followed him into the bedroom. Mrs. O'Grady lay in bed, a clean quilt covering her, a baby in her arms. She looked up when she saw Jolene and a smile illuminated her weary face. "It's a boy!"

Harp opened his eyes to hear laughter drifting into the room. Glancing around the sitting room, he saw Jolene had left. The clock said it was five minutes after midnight.

Getting up, he wandered out of the room. There was a light on in the bedroom. O'Grady was at the foot of the bed. Glancing up, he saw Harp and motioned him into the room.

Jolene glanced up, surprised to see him standing there, his hair tousled from sleep. He grinned when he saw the baby. "Glad to see the little guy made it. What's 'is name?"

"How'd you know it was a boy?" Jolene asked.

"I didn't. I'm a good guesser."

Mrs. O'Grady laughed. "His name is Curt," she said softly.

For a minute, Harp was stunned. "What? How…"

This time Mr. O'Grady laughed. "It was Jolene's idea. If it hadna been fer ye, the doc wouldna made it in time."

"I'll be," Harp said softly. But this time he wasn't looking at the baby. He was looking at Jolene.

It was two years later in late May. Jolene had just turned seventeen, and Elizabeth fifteen. The ranch had grown bigger and there were more horses. It was really paying off. So much that O'Grady was talking of hiring more hands within the next few months.

The sun was beginning to set and the supper dishes were done. Jolene stood on the bottom rail of a corral fence and watched a new filly wobble around on its long legs.

Jolene expected the tall shadow behind her and didn't even turn around. "Hello, Harp." They were no longer just friends. Their friendship had grown much stronger than that. It had grown to love.

"Howdy, Lena." Harp's hand came to rest on top of hers on the rail as he stopped beside her. For a minute, they just watched the horses in silence.

"Seems like a long time since we met," Harp said suddenly.

"Over two years." Jolene smiled. "You weren't very friendly then."

"Am I friendly now?" He was teasing.

Jolene laughed. "Most of the time," she teased back.

Their eyes met and suddenly his blue eyes turned serious. His hand tightened over hers, causing her heart to flip, and he turned so he was facing her.

"We been through a lot together," he said quietly. "An' I'd like to continue. Jolene, what would you say if I asked you to marry me?"

Jolene's heart nearly stopped. But she made up her mind quickly. "I would say yes."

His face broke into a huge grin, his blue eyes laughing again. "Would you marry me?"

Jolene's dark eyes met his. "Yes."